Ages
6-7

Disney LEARNING

P9-DNX-609

Magical Adventures
in
First Grade

Carson Dellosa Education
Greensboro, North Carolina

This workbook belongs to:

Credits: 85: © Nelson Education Ltd. 107: (dates) picturepartners/Shutterstock.com; (blue plates) Borna_Mirahmadian/Shutterstock.com. 109: (left to right) Rido/Shutterstock.com; Africa Studio/Shutterstock.com; volkovslava/Shutterstock.com; MarcusVDT/Shutterstock.com; Dorottya Mathe/Shutterstock.com; 5 second Studio/Shutterstock.com; pathdoc/Shutterstock.com; volkovslava/Shutterstock.com. 173: (toothpaste) F16-ISO100/Shutterstock.com; (paper clips) escova/Shutterstock.com; (comb) Terekhov igor/Shutterstock.com. 179: (left to right) AlenKadr/Shutterstock.com; DW labs Incorporated/Shutterstock.com; Andrey_Kuzmin/Shutterstock.com; Daria Medvedeva/Shutterstock.com; topnatthapon/Shutterstock.com; Big Pants Production/Shutterstock.com. 204: (paint cans) Brooke Becker/Shutterstock.com; (wool) Picsfive/Shutterstock.com; (baskets) Gong To/Shutterstock.com. 205: (boxes) jocic/Shutterstock.com. 208: (orange wool) Simon Mayer/Shutterstock.com; (green wool) Vasilius/Shutterstock.com; (blue wool) Nataliia K/Shutterstock.com.

Disney LEARNING

COPYRIGHT © 2020 Disney Enterprises, Inc.
All rights reserved.

Published by
Carson Dellosa Education
PO Box 35665
Greensboro, NC 27425 USA

Except as permitted under the United States Copyright Act, no part of this publication may be reproduced, stored, or distributed in any form or by any means (mechanically, electronically, recording, etc.) without the prior written consent of Carson Dellosa Education.

Printed in the USA • All rights reserved.
02-111201151

ISBN 978-1-4838-5867-8

Contents

© Disney

Dear Parent or Caregiver,

This workbook encourages your child to practice essential skills alongside their favorite Disney characters. It is designed to reinforce foundational concepts learned in school and boost your child's confidence in reading, writing, and math.

Examples and Practice: Disney characters are learning partners. They provide examples to help teach your child core concepts!

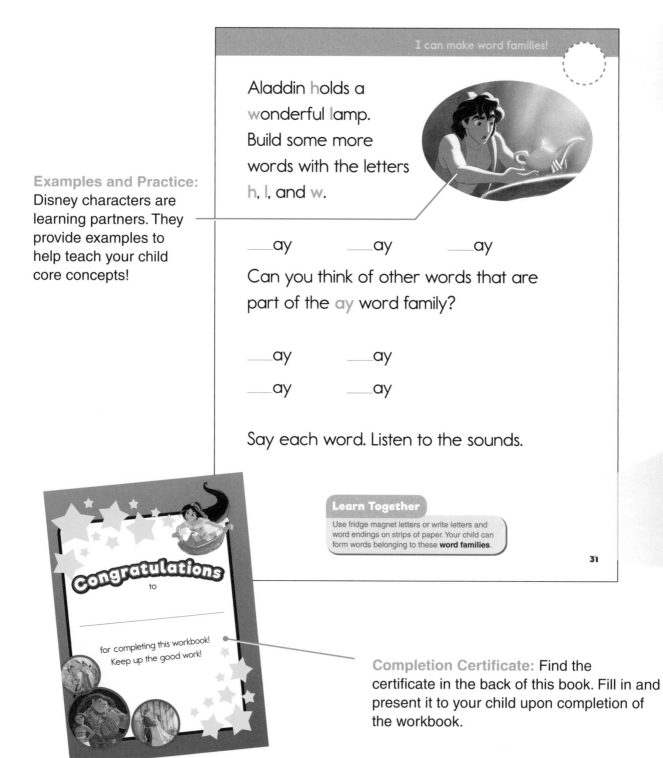

I can make word families!

Aladdin holds a wonderful lamp. Build some more words with the letters h, l, and w.

_____ay   _____ay   _____ay

Can you think of other words that are part of the ay word family?

_____ay   _____ay
_____ay   _____ay

Say each word. Listen to the sounds.

Learn Together

Use fridge magnet letters or write letters and word endings on strips of paper. Your child can form words belonging to these **word families**.

31

Congratulations
to
_____
for completing this workbook!
Keep up the good work!

Completion Certificate: Find the certificate in the back of this book. Fill in and present it to your child upon completion of the workbook.

© Disney

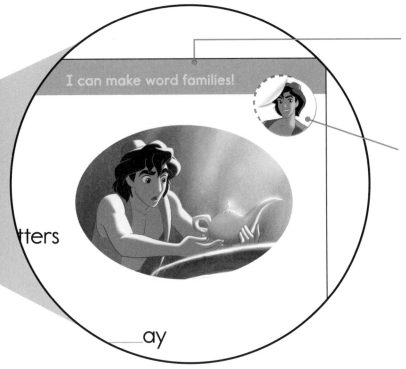

I Can: Each lesson includes an "I can" statement written in child-friendly language. It indicates what your child is able to do and can also be a learning target or goal.

Reward Stickers: To conclude each lesson, a reward sticker can be placed in the dashed red circle. Find stickers in the back of this book. The reward stickers build confidence and motivate your child.

Learn Together: Each lesson includes suggestions for additional activities that reinforce learning. These activities promote real-world connections, critical thinking, and communication skills.

Bonus Activities: Suggestions are provided beginning on page 212 to further develop and foster your child's understanding of subject areas important to school success.

Glossary: Definitions, background information, and explanations of **black bolded** terms can be found in the glossary.

Answer Key: Sample answers for activities are provided, where necessary, at the back of the book.

Happy Learning!

© Disney

What Is Your Name?

This is Rapunzel.

Rapunzel is her name.

Print your name. Make sure to capitalize the first letter.

Learn Together

Your child may need help spelling or printing their first and last name. Help your child add an "I can ..." sentence to their picture (I can dance; I can read).

6

© Disney

Draw a picture of yourself. Print your name below your picture.

© Disney

A, B, C, and D

Trace and print the letters.

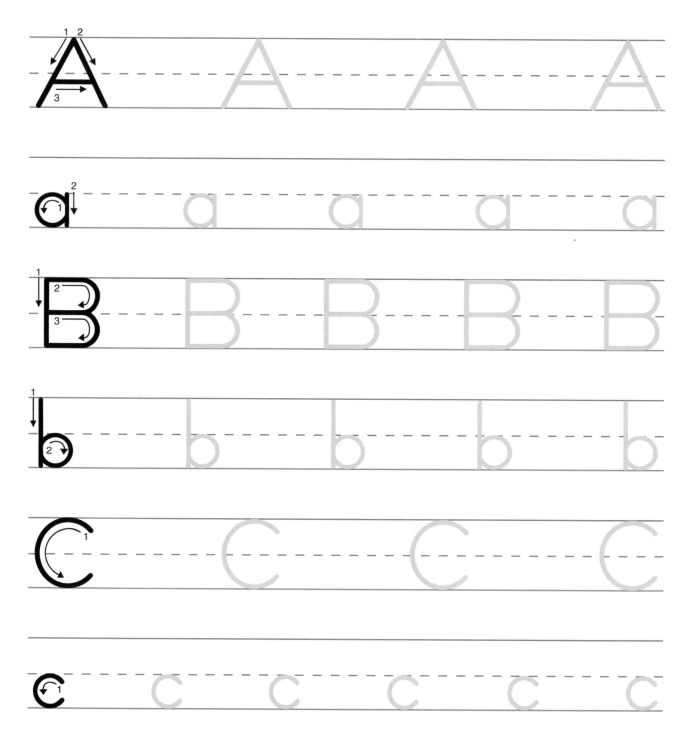

© Disney

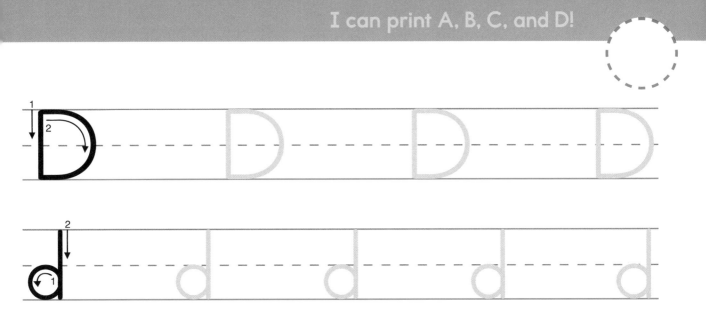

Trace the missing letters.

Belle and the

Beast dance.

Learn Together

As your child reads the sentence above, they can listen to the sounds the letters make. Use your finger to trace the letters **a**, **b**, **c**, and **d** on your child's hand. Can they identify the letters?

© Disney

E, F, G, and H

Trace and print the letters.

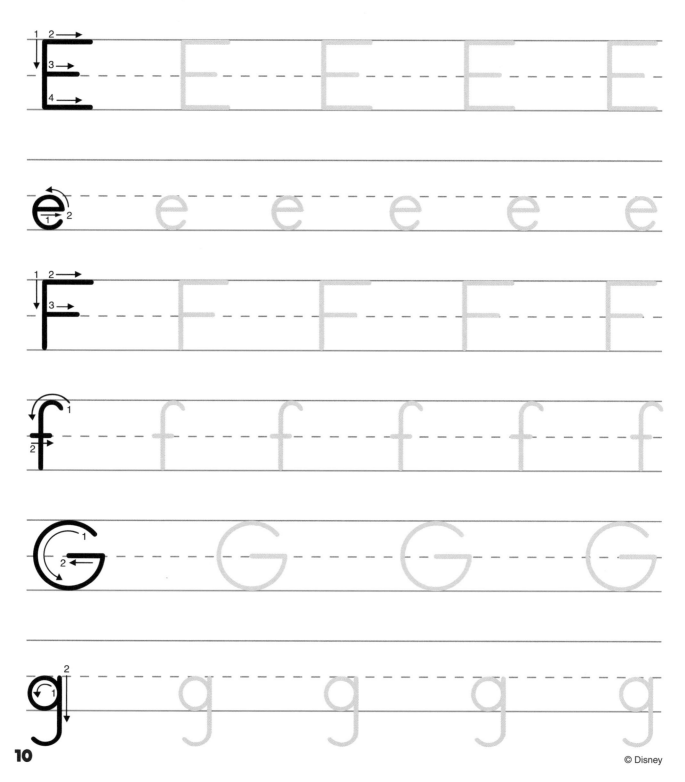

© Disney

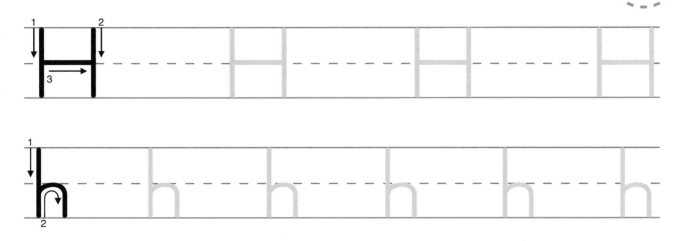

Trace the missing letters.

Aladdin escapes
from the guards.

Learn Together

Your child can use materials, such as modeling
clay, to practice forming the letters **e**, **f**, **g**, and **h**.

© Disney

I, J, K, and L

Trace and print the letters.

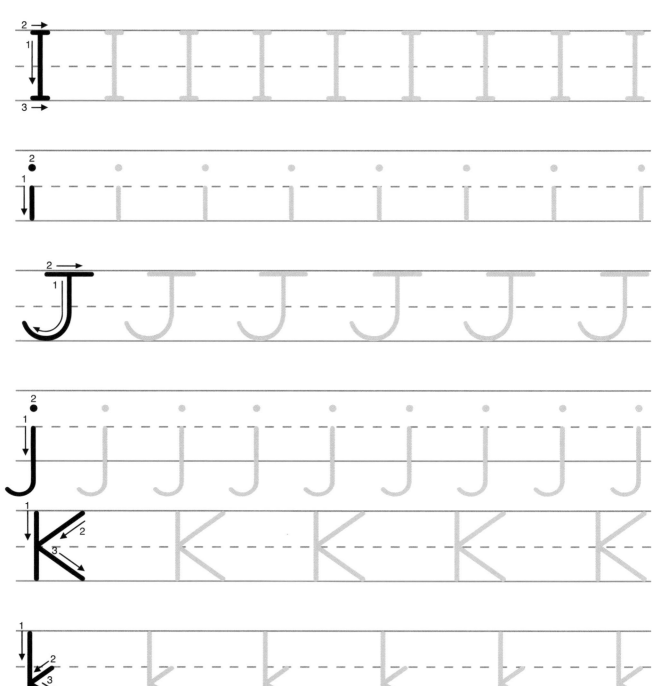

© Disney

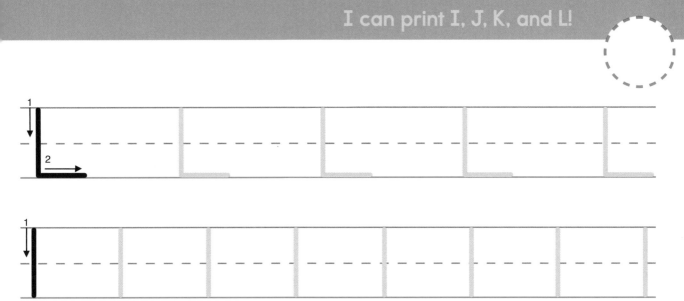

Trace the missing letters.

Judy and Nick

solve cases.

Learn Together

Your child can trace these letters with a finger. Talk about how the letters are formed (the letter I has one downward stroke).

© Disney

M, N, O, and P

Trace and print the letters.

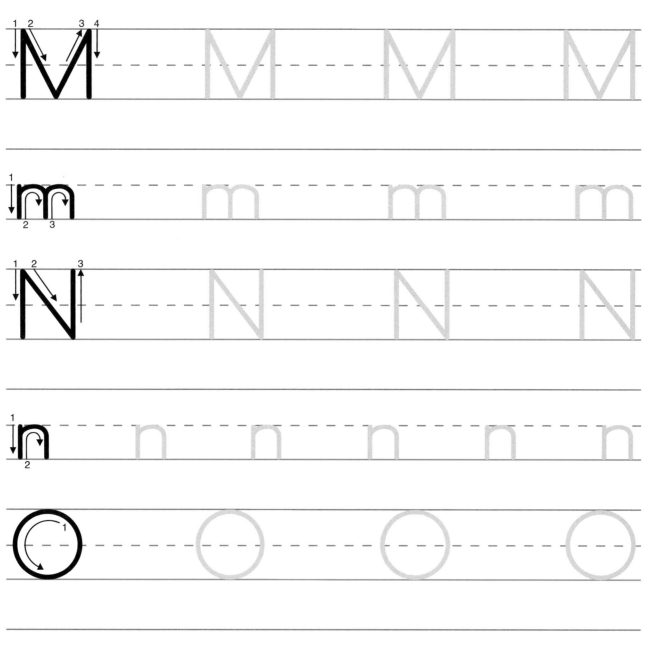

© Disney

P P P P P

p p p p p

Trace the missing letters.

Moana holds the

pounamu stone.

Learn Together

With your child, look at maps or globes.
Find words that start with **M**, **N**, **O**, or **P**
(Mexico, North, Ocean, Pacific).

© Disney

Q, R, S, and T

Trace and print the letters.

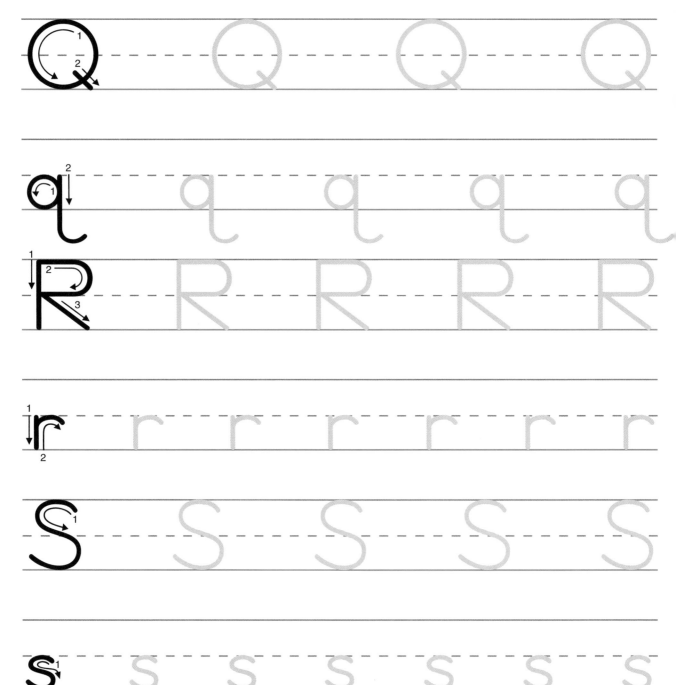

© Disney

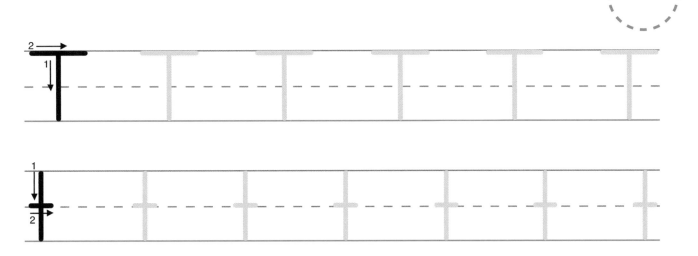

T

t

Trace the missing letters.

Rapunzel stares

at the queen.

© Disney

Learn Together

Work with your child to compose another sentence
about Rapunzel, using the letters **q, r, s**, and **t**
(**T**he **q**ueen welcome**s R**apunzel back.).

U, V, W, and X

Trace and print the letters.

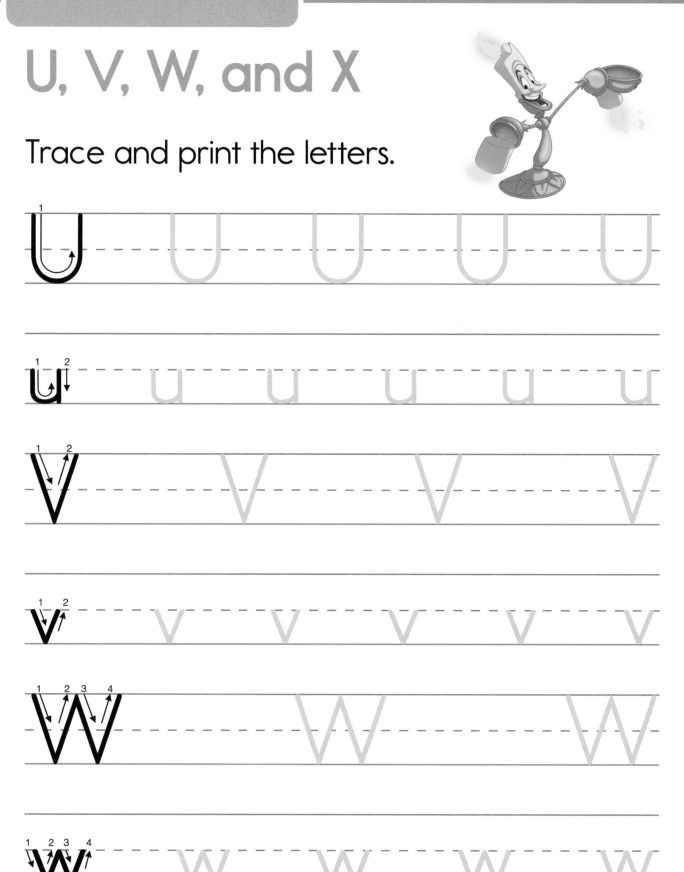

© Disney

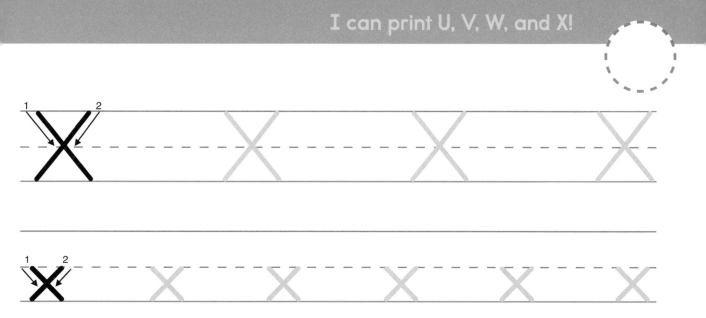

X X X X

X X X X X X

Trace the missing letters.

Wolves box in

Maurice.

Learn Together

Your child can look for the letters **u**, **v**, **w**, and **x** in signs and labels. Encourage your child to trace these letters with a finger, following the path they would use to write the letter.

© Disney

Y and Z

Trace and print the letters.

© Disney

Trace the missing letters.

Judy finally goes
to Zootopia.

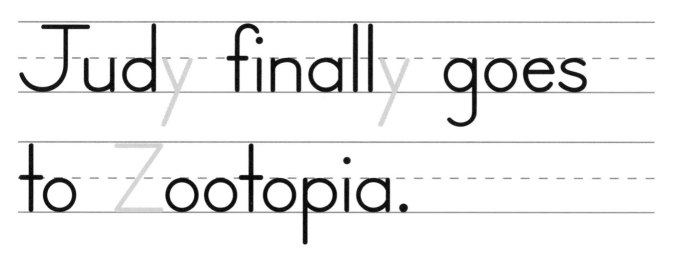

Learn Together

Sing the alphabet song with your child. Pause now
and then for your child to supply the next letter.

© Disney

The Case of the Missing Letters

Nick is looking for clues.

Fill in the missing letters.

A B C __ E F G __ I J K __ M

N O __ Q R S __ U V W __ Y Z

© Disney

Fill in the missing letters.

a b __ d e __ g h __ j k __ m

n __ p q __ s t __ v w __ y z

Learn Together

Provide opportunities for your child to learn **alphabetical order**. Cover up a letter and ask, "What letter is missing?" Name a letter and ask, "Which letter comes after this one? Which letter comes before it?" Take turns with your child.

© Disney

Matching Letters

The letters in the library are a mess.

Match up the letters.

The first one has been done for you.

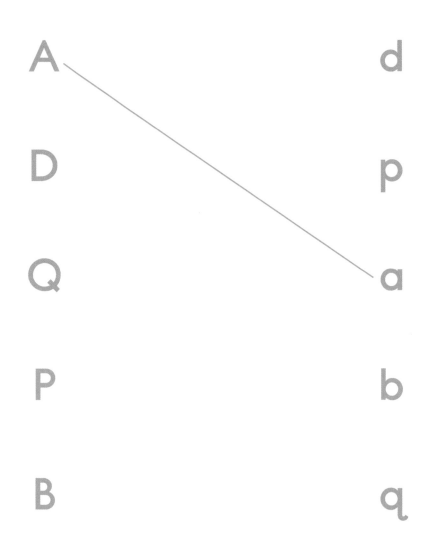

A   d

D   p

Q   a

P   b

B   q

© Disney

Now, match up these letters.

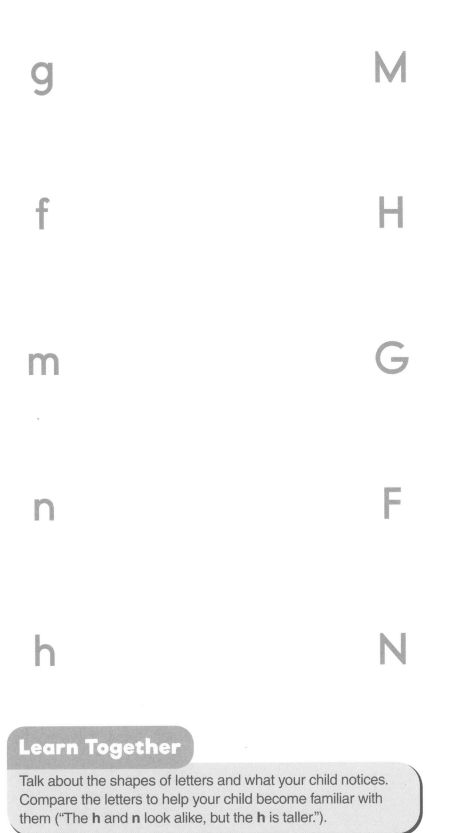

g   M

f   H

m   G

n   F

h   N

Learn Together

Talk about the shapes of letters and what your child notices.
Compare the letters to help your child become familiar with
them ("The **h** and **n** look alike, but the **h** is taller.").

© Disney

Princess Puzzle Time!

P is for pan!

Listen to the sound made by the letter p at the start of each word.

Add the letter p to make words.

____et   ____ot   ____up   ____it

The letter p can also come at the end of a word to make the end sound.

Add the letter p to make words.

na____   ho____   si____   pu____

Say the words. Listen to the sound made by the letter p.

© Disney

Complete each sentence by adding the letter p.

Rapunzel makes ___erfect ___uzzles.

She ___aints ___urple flowers.

Will she lea___ out of the tower?

Flynn will hel___ her escape.

Read each sentence. Listen for the sound the letter p makes.

Learn Together

Help your child read, emphasizing the sound of the letter **p**. Focus on initial and final **letter sounds** in other simple words. Your child may be ready to identify the sound made by **p**, or other letters, in the middle of a word (Ra**p**unzel).

© Disney

In the Family

You can add p to an to make pan.
Add c, t, v, and m to an to make new words.
Say each word out loud.

can   tan   van   man

These words are all part of the an word
family. Can you think of other words that are
part of this family?

___an   ___an   ___an

Add letters to make words that belong
to the op **word family**.

___op   ___op   ___op   ___op

© Disney

Add letters to make words that belong to the at word family.

＿＿at   ＿＿at   ＿＿at   ＿＿at

Can you think of other words that are part of this family?

＿＿at   ＿＿at   ＿＿at

Add letters to make words that belong to the ug word family.

＿＿ug   ＿＿ug   ＿＿ug   ＿＿ug

Learn Together

Help your child read these words, emphasizing their sounds.
Use the words to make silly sentences (Hug the bug on the rug.).
Make other words with these and other word families.

© Disney

More Words, Please!

This magic scarab is no ordinary bug!
Build some more words with the letters b, m, and n.

___et   ___et   ___et

Can you think of other words that are part of the et word family?

___et   ___et

___et   ___et

Say each word. Listen to the sounds.

© Disney

Aladdin holds a wonderful lamp. Build some more words with the letters h, l, and w.

___ay   ___ay   ___ay

Can you think of other words that are part of the ay word family?

___ay   ___ay

___ay   ___ay

Say each word. Listen to the sounds.

Learn Together

Use fridge magnet letters or write letters and word endings on strips of paper. Your child can form words belonging to these word families.

© Disney

Working Together

Judy and Nick learn to work together. Some letters work together too. For example, the b and l in blue work together. Say the word. Listen to the sound bl makes at the beginning of the word.

Build some words using letters that work together.

sl   bl   fl

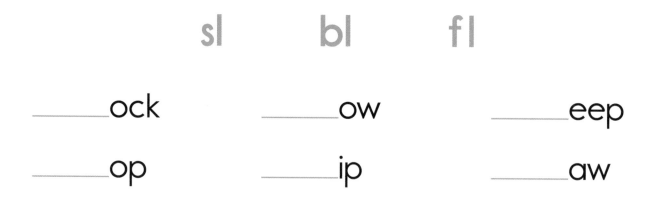

_____ock   _____ow   _____eep

_____op   _____ip   _____aw

Say each word you made.

© Disney

Nick and Judy help each other to the very end. Some letters help each other to create a single sound.

Build some words using letters that work together.

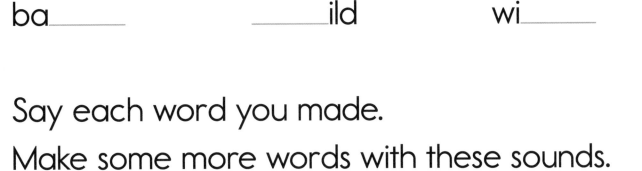

ch	sh	th	wh

_____air   fi_____   _____ale

ba_____   _____ild   wi_____

Say each word you made.
Make some more words with these sounds.

Learn Together

Help your child work out which of the **blends** or **digraphs** to add. If they add the wrong one, say the word with your child, and ask if they think it sounds right. Note that more than one **letter combination** may work. Experiment with other letter combinations.

© Disney

Short and Long

Vowels help you make words. Some vowels make a **short vowel sound**. The a in hat and the u in nut are short vowels.

Add the missing vowels to the sentences below.

Moana holds a special r____ck in her h____nd.

The p____g is in the n____t.

Read the sentences out loud. Listen to the vowel sounds.

© Disney

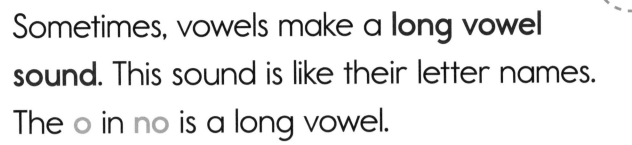

Sometimes, vowels make a **long vowel sound.** This sound is like their letter names. The o in no is a long vowel.

Underline the vowel in each word that makes the long vowel sound.

wake   he   like   bone   use   gold   be   so

Say each word.

Learn Together

Play "Short or Long?" with your child. List words that have a short vowel sound (cup, rug) or a long vowel sound (bike, home). Take turns saying words. Help your child identify vowel sounds as short or long.

© Disney

Team Work!

Judy and Nick are a team. Like Judy and Nick, sometimes vowels work together as a team. You only hear one sound. Team has a long e sound.

Underline the vowel letters in each word. Write the long vowel sound you hear.

beet ___   bead ___   wait ___

need ___   boat ___   goal ___

meat ___   bait ___

© Disney

The letter e at the end of a word can make the vowel in the middle long. For example, add e to the word pin to make pine. The short i sound in pin becomes a long vowel sound.

Add an e to the end of the words below.

cop___   tim___   cap___

rat___   cam___   bit___

cut___   din___

Say each word out loud.
Listen to the vowel sound.

Learn Together

Discuss how "When two vowels go walking, the first vowel does the talking" and how a silent (or magic) **e** can make a short vowel long. Work with your child to list other words using these rules (feed, dream, coat, like, bike, use, rope).

© Disney

Words I Know

There are some words you will read often.
We call those words **sight words.**

Read these sight words out loud.

he   they   her

          she   him   them

          © Disney

Fill in the missing sight words.

Rapunzel uses _____ hair to escape the tower.

Outside, _____ is filled with joy.

Flynn thinks _____ should go back.

Rapunzel does not agree with _____.

So _____ comes up with a plan.

But is it the best plan for both of _____?

Learn Together

Help your child read the sight words, noting the letters they begin with and how long each word is. Your child can circle any other words they already know in the sentences.

© Disney

More Words I Know

Do you see how Heihei likes to play?

Does the coconut make Heihei look silly?

Will Pua get Heihei to stop?

Read these sight words out loud.

make   play   stop

look   see

© Disney

<u>Underline</u> the sight words below.

Little Moana loves to play.

She can see a turtle on the beach.

Moana takes a closer look.

She helps the turtle make it to safety.

Moana can stop the birds from getting the turtle.

Learn Together

Help your child read each sentence, pausing at each sight word to let them read it. Make flash cards with some of the sight words (see the list in the glossary). Ask your child to read the words and use them in sentences.

© Disney

I Am Ready to Read!

Nick works with Judy to solve cases.

He is very smart.

That will help them, because some cases are hard.

Read these sight words out loud.

because   with   that

very   some

© Disney

Fill in the missing sight words.

Judy and Nick find s _ _ _ _ _ clues.

Nick runs v _ _ _ _ fast
w _ _ _ _ _ Judy.

Judy makes a call
b _ _ _ _ _ _ _ _ _ they need help.

They tell the police t _ _ _ _ _ they
have new clues.

Learn Together

Ask your child to choose two sight words
from this page. With your child, make up a
sentence that includes the two words.

© Disney

I Am Reading!

Can Belle save the Beast?

Is she strong enough?

He will be changed.

They are going to be together.

Read these sight words out loud.

is   will   are

        can   be

© Disney

Fill in the missing sight words.

How _____ Belle save the Beast?

Belle _____ save him with her love.

They will ____ ____ happy soon, after the Beast

____ ____ changed.

Belle and the Beast ____ ____ ____ in love.

Learn Together

On a blank piece of paper, create three columns. Label them *characters*, *setting*, and *plot*. With your child, fill out the columns with details from the story above.

© Disney

Rhyme Time

Rhyming words have letters at the end that sound the same.

Circle the words that rhyme.

sea   tea   flea   sit   hit   fit

line   fine   mine

Say the words out loud. Listen to the rhyme.

© Disney

Read these sentences out loud.

<u>Underline</u> the words that rhyme.

Heihei moves fast.

He flies up the mast.

The mast is tall.

Will Heihei fall?

The sea is rough.

Moana has had enough.

Learn Together

With your child, make flash cards with simple one-syllable rhyming words (slow/flow, cat/hat, car/bar). Put one word on the front of each card and one or more rhyming words on the back.

© Disney

Words That Sound the Same

Some words sound the same but are spelled with different letters.

Say these words out loud.

Circle the groups of words that sound the same.

see   sea   two   too   to

four   for   tail   tale   I   eye

© Disney

Trace the words that complete each sentence. Read the sentence out loud.

Jasmine gives two gifts to Aladdin.

For Genie, four wishes are too many to grant.

Rajah the tiger has a tail. Aladdin has a tale to tell.

Learn Together

Ask your child to make up a sentence for each pair of **homophones**. Point to the word when it is said.

© Disney

Multiple Meanings

Words can even be spelled the same but have different meanings. You have to read the sentence carefully to know which meaning is being used.

Nick has to train to be a police officer.
(to learn something by doing it over and over)

Judy rides the train.
(a long line of cars that run on a track)

Circle the definition being used for the word cold.

It is going to be cold this weekend.

1. having a low temperature; not warm

2. an illness that often includes a cough, sore throat, and runny nose

© Disney

Circle the correct definition of the colored word in each sentence.

Airplanes fly at high speeds.

a small insect with two wings

to move through the air

May I pet your dog?

an animal that lives with people

to touch or stroke

Swing the bat to hit the ball.

a small, flying mammal

a wooden stick used in baseball

Nick likes spending time in parks.

open, grassy areas for relaxing

stops and leaves a car

Learn Together

Give your child another word that has more than one meaning but the same spelling, like *fair* (equal or a place with rides and games). Have your child come up with a sentence for each meaning. Do this with other words as well.

© Disney

Seeing Base Words

Rapunzel and Flynn are unlikely friends. Like is the **base word** of unlikely.

Underline the base words.

longest   darker

retell   preview

© Disney

Match each new beginning to a base word.

re   able

un   read

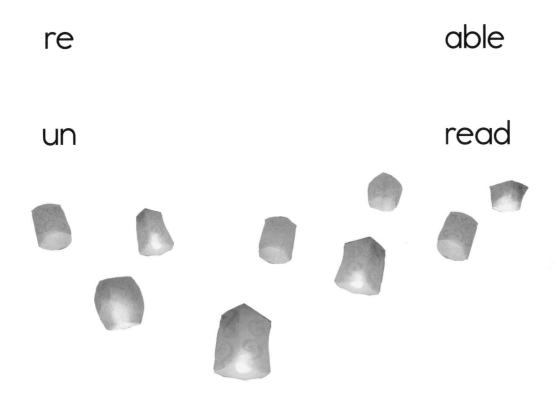

Match each base word to a new ending.

sing   er

jump   ed

Learn Together

Explain to your child the meaning of **prefix** and **suffix**. Point to the new words created on this page as examples. *Re* and *un* are prefixes because they come at the beginning of the words, and *er* and *ed* are suffixes because they come at the end.

© Disney

I Know Nouns

A noun names a person, place, or thing. A **proper noun** names a specific person, place, or thing. Proper nouns are capitalized. **Common nouns** are not.

Underline the proper nouns. Circle the common nouns.

Agrabah   city   princess

Aladdin   monkey   Abu

© Disney

Read the sentences below. (Circle) the proper nouns that should be capitalized.

jasmine is playing with her pet tiger rajah.

The monkey abu shares a loaf of bread with aladdin.

The cave of wonders holds a treasure jafar wants.

Learn Together

Ask your child to name familiar people, places, and things. Be sure they name both common nouns and proper nouns. Make flash cards out of the nouns your child names. Ask your child to sort the flash cards into two groups: common and proper nouns.

One or Many?

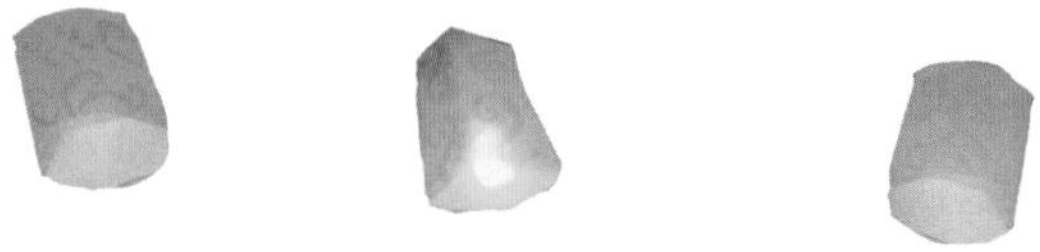

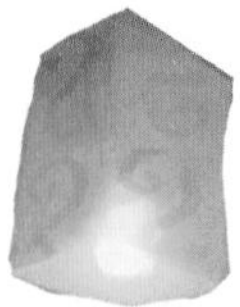

A **singular noun** names one person, place, or thing. A **plural noun** names more than one. Plural nouns often end in s.

Add **s** to the nouns below to make them plural.

lantern   _____

guard   _____

horse   _____

boat   _____

cave   _____

flower   _____

© Disney

Look at the pictures. (Circle) the correct singular or plural noun.

pan

pans

lantern

lanterns

paintbrush

paintbrushes

person

people

Learn Together

Ask your child to identify the singular and plural forms of other nouns that name things around you. Be sure to prompt the inclusion of some plural nouns that do not end in **s**, such as **children**, **feet**, or **mice**.

© Disney

Whose Is That?

Make the nouns below **possessive** by adding 's.

Moana_____ boat

Maui_____ fishhook

Motunui_____ chief

Te Fiti_____ heart

The ocean_____ chosen one

© Disney

Add an apostrophe to the possessive nouns.

One day, Moana will be Motunui☐s chief.

A camakau is a voyager☐s ship.

Moana and Maui have to enter Tamatoa☐s lair.

Moana restores Te Fiti☐s heart.

Learn Together

A possessive noun is a noun that shows ownership. Have your child make a list of things around them. Ask your child to make up a sentence showing who each object belongs to.

© Disney

Replacing Nouns

A **pronoun** is a word that takes the place of a noun.

the pronoun that can take the place of each underlined noun.

Judy heads to work.

She/It

Nick asks Judy for help with a case.

I/He

Nick and Judy are excited to solve the case.

Them/They

© Disney

Replace the word or words with a pronoun.

them   him   her

Nick is looking for Judy.

_____

Nick is waiting for Flash.

_____

Chief Bogo tells Judy and Nick to get

on the case! _____

Learn Together

With your child, go back and read the sentences on page 55.
Point to a couple different nouns. Ask your child to choose a
pronoun to take the place of those nouns.

© Disney

That's Mine!

A possessive pronoun is a pronoun that shows ownership. Some examples of possessive pronouns are:

your	yours	my	mine
their	theirs	our	ours

© Disney

Choose a possessive pronoun from page 62 to complete the sentences.

Belle asks Gaston, "May I have

_____ book back?"

The villagers make _____ way to the castle.

Belle loves the library, so Beast says, "Then it's

_____."

Lumière says to Cogsworth, "She's

_____ guest."

Learn Together

Help your child work out which possessive pronoun to use. Explain that there could be more than one right answer, depending on who the speaker is talking to and about. Practice using possessive pronouns in new sentences you come up with together.

© Disney

Subject-Verb Agreement

When a sentence is about one person or thing, add s to the verb.

Jasmine rides the magic carpet.

When a sentence is about more than one person or thing, do not add s.

Jasmine and Aladdin ride the magic carpet.

© Disney

Match each sentence to the correct ending.

Rajah

bite a suitor's pants.

bites a suitor's pants.

Jafar

tricks the sultan.

trick the sultan.

The guards

captures Aladdin.

capture Aladdin.

Learn Together

Create sentences about your child or about both of you. Have your child fill in the correct verb that agrees with the subject.

© Disney

What's Happening?

Verbs have different tenses. They can tell us what's happening now, what has happened in the past, and what will happen in the future.

Look at these verbs.

Present Tense:

Jasmine and Aladdin f ly on a magic carpet.

Past Tense:

Abu stole a loaf of bread.

Future Tense:

Jasmine will be the ruler of Agrabah.

© Disney

Read the sentences below. (Circle) the present tense verbs, draw a [box] around the past tense verbs, and <u>underline</u> the future tense verbs.

Jasmine snuck into the city.

Aladdin rubs the lamp and releases the Genie.

The Genie will help Aladdin become a prince.

Iago stole the lamp.

Learn Together

Ask your child to make up three sentences, one for each **verb tense**: one with present tense verbs, one with past tense verbs, and one with future tense verbs. Help them out if they get stuck.

© Disney

Combining Sentences

Sometimes, sentences can be combined.

The table was set.
The table was filled with food.

Both sentences tell about the table. You can combine the sentences using and.

The table was set and filled with food.

Place a check mark next to the sentences that use and.

☐ Lumiére likes to sing.
☐ Lumiére likes to dance.
☐ Lumiére likes to sing and dance.

☐ Beast is kind.
☐ Beast and Mrs. Potts are kind.
☐ Mrs. Potts is kind.

© Disney

Combine each pair of sentences into one sentence. Write the new sentence.

Mrs. Potts likes tea. Chip likes tea.

_____

_____

Maurice rides horses. Belle rides horses.

_____

_____

Beast is under a spell. The servants are under a spell.

_____

_____

Learn Together

Ask your child to think of two things that are the same in some way. They might be the same color or same size. Write the pair of sentences your child comes up with. Then, ask your child to combine the sentences using **and**.

© Disney

69

Pictures Tell the Tale

© Disney

Circle what Rapunzel is looking at.

Describe how Rapunzel is feeling.

_____

_____

_____

Describe the setting.

_____

_____

_____

Learn Together

With your child, examine and discuss this picture. What else does your child notice? When you read books together, encourage your child to use the picture clues to help them understand the story.

© Disney

I Know How That Feels

© Disney

Moana and Heihei are on the boat.

The waves are very big.

Heihei holds on tightly.

They do their best to stay afloat as they flee from Te Kā.

The waves are getting higher.

How would you feel if you were on the boat with Moana and Heihei? Why?

_____

_____

_____

Learn Together

Read the story to your child. Help your child **make connections** and respond to the questions. Ask your child to recall a time when they were challenged (swimming for the first time). How did they feel?

© Disney

Belle and Her Prince Dance

© Disney

The Beast becomes a prince.

The prince is a tall man.

He has brown hair and a kind smile.

Belle wears a yellow dress to dance with him.

The prince is very gentle with Belle.

Underline the clues in the story that help you answer these questions.

Is the prince tall or short?

What does Belle wear for their dance?

Learn Together

With your child, describe what a favorite character from a book or movie looks like.

© Disney

Beginning, Middle, …

A story has a beginning.

Things happen in the middle of the story.

And then the story ends.

© Disney

Read the story on pages 77 and 78.
Look for the beginning, middle, and end.

One day, Judy hears a cry of "Thief!"
She sprints to the rescue!

She chases the thief, a weasel,
through Little Rodentia.

There are small rodents out shopping
everywhere.

She does not want to lose the weasel,
but she does not want to step on
anyone.

(To be continued)

Learn Together

Read the story to your child. Help them identify **key details**. They can use the picture and text to help them. Read the rest of this story on page 78.

© Disney

...and End

(Continued from page 77)

Judy <u>dodges</u> rodents and flying donuts to try to catch the weasel.

Finally, Judy catches up to the weasel! She <u>slams</u> a runaway donut over his head.

Judy brings the weasel down to the station. She proves she is a good cop!

© Disney

Learn Together

Read the story to your child. Pause at the underlined words and ask if they know the word's meaning. If not, ask them to use **context clues** to guess the meaning.

© Disney

Order! Order!

Put the story back in order.

Number the boxes in the order the story happened.

Judy chases the thief.

Judy hears someone cry, "Thief!"

© Disney

Finally, she gets the weasel and brings him to the station.

There are small rodents everywhere, and Judy has to dodge them.

Learn Together

Help your child figure out the story order. Find other pictures for your child to put in order. Encourage them to sequence other objects or actions.

© Disney

What Do I Know?

Moana's Polynesian island is surrounded by coral reefs.

© Disney

Fish, turtles, crabs, and many other animals live in the coral reefs.

Coral reefs provide shelter and food to these animals.

Many of the animals in the Polynesian reef do not live anywhere else in the world.

Write one fact you learned about reefs.

_____

_____

Learn Together

Read this **nonfiction text** to your child. Ask your child what differences there are between this text and the **fiction** text on pages 77 and 78.

© Disney

Where Do I Go?

Maps are pictures that can tell you what a community looks like.

Trace a path from the A in Tundratown to the B in the Rainforest District.

The Regions of Zootopia

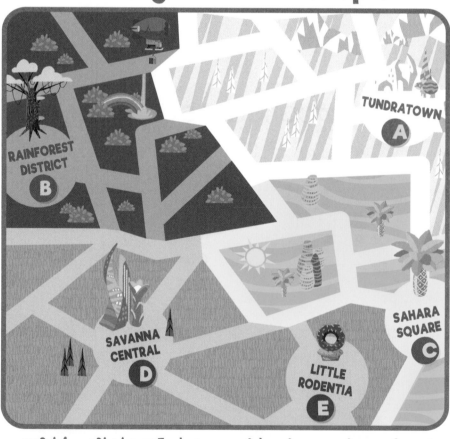

■ Rainforest District ■ Tundratown ■ Sahara Square ■ Savanna Central

© Disney

Here is a map that shows some of the things that might be in your neighborhood.

Put an X beside places on this map that are in your neighborhood.

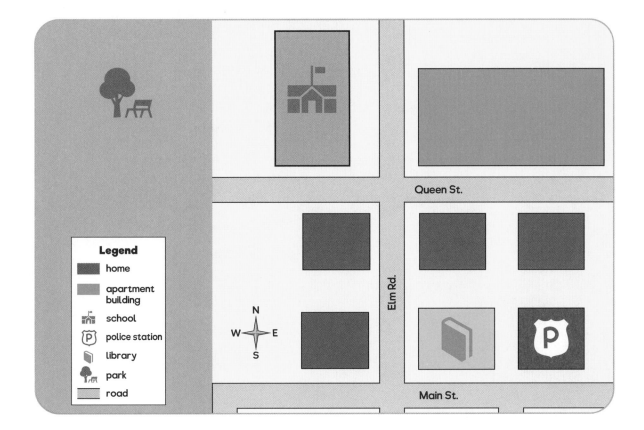

Trace a path from the library to the park.

Learn Together

Examine the maps with your child. Talk about what the maps show and the features they use (symbols, labels, lines). With your child, create a map of your neighborhood.

© Disney

What Is It Like?

© Disney

The magic carpet is made of soft, colorful wool.

It is purple with gold and red patterns.

It can move on its own!

When it flies, it rustles and hums, soaring and diving.

Underline the words that describe what the magic carpet looks like.

Circle a word that describes what the carpet feels like.

Learn Together

These description words are **adjectives**. What other adjectives would your child add? Your child can try describing Aladdin or Abu.

© Disney

Rapunzel's Hair

© Disney

Rapunzel's hair has healing power.

She is locked up in a tower.

Flynn cuts her hair with his knife.

He wants her to have her own life.

Rapunzel's tears hold the power of the sun

and save the day for everyone.

Draw a star beside your favorite part of the poem.

Learn Together

Read the poem to your child. Help your child find the rhythm by pointing out the rhyming words and clapping to the beat. Read the poem again, pointing out that each clap is a **syllable**. Explain that every syllable needs a vowel.

© Disney

What Is the Title?

A title tells you what a story is about.

Books, poems, movies, and plays all have titles.

The title of this book is *Belle to the Rescue.*

Write another title for this book.

_____

_____

_____

© Disney

Look at this picture.

Think about the story it tells.

Write a title for this story.

_____

_____

Learn Together

Help your child print the titles they have composed. Ask, "Why did you choose those titles?" Help your child brainstorm ideas for titles as they write their own stories.

© Disney

Label It!

Labels give you information about what is in a picture.

What do the labels tell you about this picture?

ticket book

police uniform

meter

safety vest

© Disney

Label this picture.

FREQUENT STOPS

Learn Together

Help your child label this picture, naming each object to label, sounding out the word, and helping them spell it. With your child, draw a picture of a neighborhood park and label it.

© Disney

Capture It with Captions

A **caption** tells you what is happening in a picture.

What do the captions tell you about these pictures?

Moana battles the Kakamora.

The Kakamora attack Maui.

© Disney

Write a caption for each picture.

© Disney

Learn Together

With your child, draw a picture. Discuss what is happening in it. Write a caption for the picture.

Lots of Sentences

A sentence tells you something.

A sentence can have different kinds of punctuation.

Belle likes to read books.

| A sentence starts with a capital letter. | This sentence ends with a period. |

Write a sentence about something you like to do.

End the sentence with a period.

_____

_____

© Disney

A sentence can ask a question.

A sentence can also show excitement.

Where is Belle going?

> A question ends with a question mark.

Belle rides fast!

> An exclamation mark shows excitement.

Write a sentence that asks a question.

_____

Write a sentence that shows excitement.

_____

Learn Together

Help your child write different sentences about your family. One sentence can end with a period, another with a question mark, and the third with an exclamation point.

© Disney

Super Stories

A story has characters, a setting, and a problem.

Judy Hopps is the first bunny to join the police force in Zootopia.

She teams up with Nick Wilde to find a missing otter. They follow clues. Sometimes, they are in danger!

Judy and Nick solve the case by working together.

© Disney

Look at the picture.
Write a story about it.

_____

_____

_____

_____

_____

_____

Learn Together

Help your child identify the setting, characters, and problem on page 98. Then help your child write a story about the picture above. Discuss the characters, the setting, and the problem.

© Disney

Dear...

A letter is a note you write to be read by someone.

Rapunzel saves Flynn's life.

Below is a letter he might write to say thank you.

Dear Rapunzel,

Start your letter with a greeting.

You saved my life!

Thank you so much.

A letter includes a message.

We will have many new adventures together.

Love,
Flynn

Always sign your name.

© Disney

Write a letter to someone special.

You can thank them for being kind.

_____

_____

_____

_____

_____

_____

Learn Together

Help your child write their letter. Discuss what makes the
person kind. Include those ideas in the letter. Create another
copy of the letter, including a date. Mail the letter.

© Disney

A Short Pause

A comma shows a short pause in a sentence.
Commas are also used in a series, or list
of words.

Read these sentences out loud. Pay attention
to the commas.

> This is a comma.

When Aladdin rubs the lamp, a genie appears.

Luckily, Aladdin knows just what he wants.

Aladdin, Genie, and Abu set off
on an adventure.

© Disney

Finish the sentences with lists of at least three words each.

Use a comma after each word in a series except the last word.

To get ready, I _____

_____

I like to eat _____

_____

My favorite movies are _____

_____

I like to play _____

_____

Learn Together

Help your child write a short story about their school day. Use commas to show pauses and series.

© Disney

Short Stuff

A **contraction** is two words put together. An apostrophe replaces the missing letters.

This is an apostrophe.

I'm is a contraction that means I am.

Underline the words that have been put together in these sentences.

That's a fun carrot pen Nick is holding.

That is   That will   That have

It's a hard case they must solve.

I have   It is   It will

© Disney

Match these contractions with the words that have been put together.

it's   she is

we're   they are

she's   it is

they're   we are

Learn Together

Look for other contractions as you read. Help your child read them and figure out what words have been put together.

© Disney

Nothing at All

The genie is out of the lamp.

The lamp has no genies in it.

You can say this another way:

The lamp has zero genies.

Zero or 0 is a number
that represents nothing.

Trace the number.

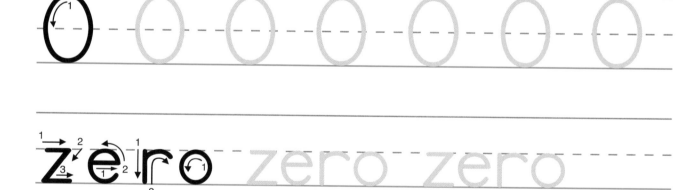

© Disney

Write 0 above the empty containers.

Learn Together

Make sure your child has an understanding of zero. Provide them with opportunities to discuss how there are zero cookies left in the box or zero toys on the floor.

© Disney

One to One

Aladdin and Jasmine each have good friends.

Draw a line from Aladdin and Jasmine to their friends.

© Disney

Draw a line to match each picture on the left with a picture on the right.

© Disney

Learn Together

Help your child identify other common examples of **one-to-one correspondence**. Match one bowl to one spoon or one mitten to its mate.

1 to 10

Rewrite these number words in order.

two   one   three

_____

five   three   four

_____

© Disney

seven   six   five

---

seven   six   eight

---

ten   eight   nine

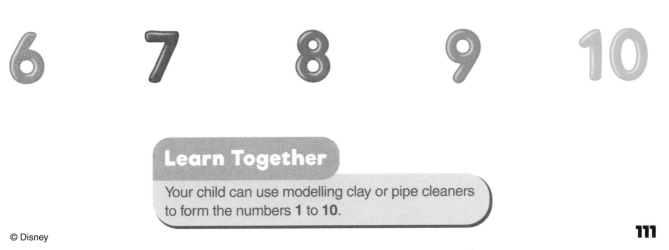

Learn Together

Your child can use modelling clay or pipe cleaners to form the numbers **1** to **10**.

© Disney

11 and 12

Moana sees 11 birds attacking a turtle.

Trace the number.

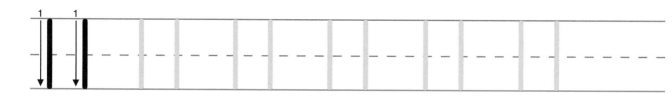

© Disney

There are 12 boats sailing.

Trace the number.

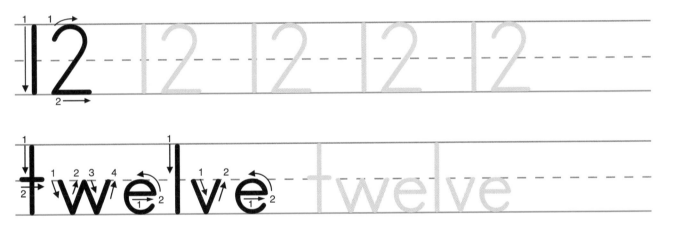

© Disney

Learn Together

Your child should be working fluently with numbers 0 to 20. When they have completed this page and the following number tracing pages, challenge your child to write numerals and number words within 120.

13 and 14

Nick has 13 stacks of cash.

Trace the number.

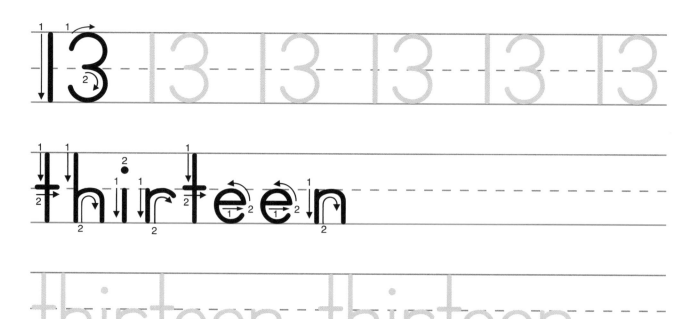

© Disney

Nick has 14 customers.

Trace the number.

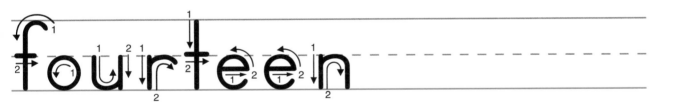

fourteen

fourteen

© Disney

Learn Together

With your child, count the bundles of cash and then the customers.
Pause now and then to let your child say the next number.

115

15 and 16

Rapunzel sees 15 flags.

Trace the number.

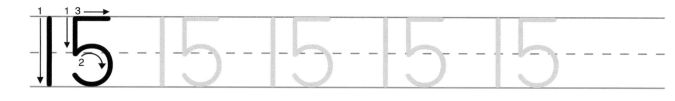

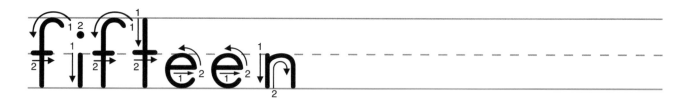

© Disney

Rapunzel sees 16 lanterns.

Trace the number.

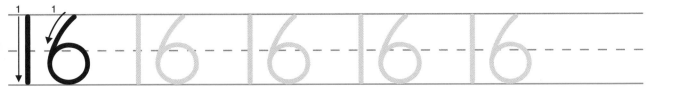

sixteen

Learn Together

Ask your child to write a number in a notebook and then draw a matching number of images.

© Disney

17 and 18

Jasmine releases 17 birds.

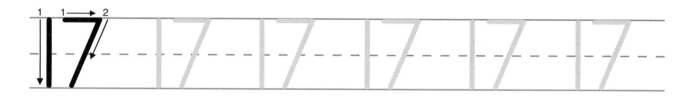

Trace the number.

17 17 17 17 17 17

seventeen

seventeen

© Disney

Now there are 18 birds.

Trace the number.

18 18 18 18 18

eighteen

eighteen

Learn Together

Discuss what your child notices about the numbers **10** through **19** (the number 1 before the second digit; the numbers are in the same order as the numbers 1 to 9). Connect this to their understanding of numbers and their understanding of ones and tens.

© Disney

19 and 20

Belle sees 19 dandelions.

Trace the number.

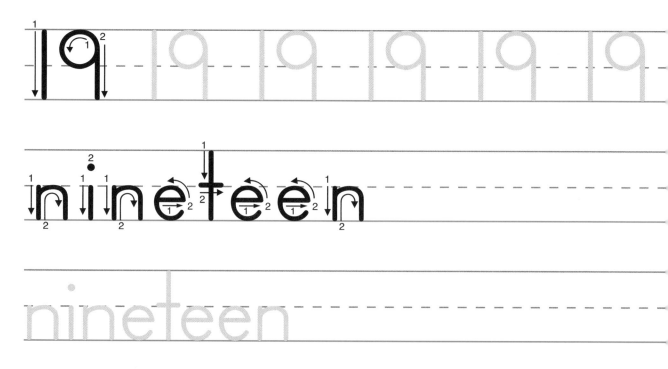

© Disney

The Beast has 20 birds.

Trace the number.

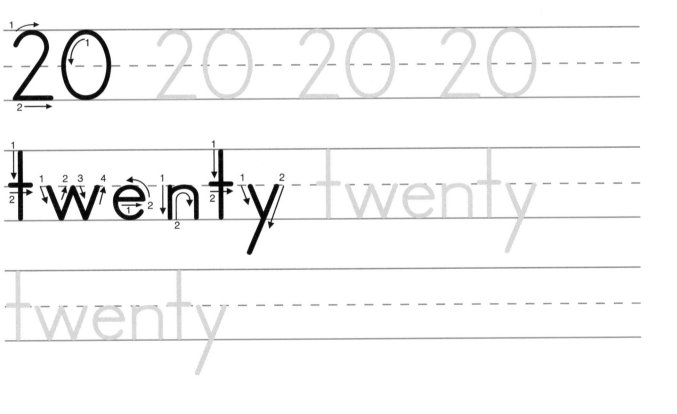

© Disney

Learn Together

With your child, take turns counting objects or steps. Try to reach 120. Challenge them by starting at a number other than 1.

On the Line

On this **number line**, show how many pictures Gramma Tala is holding.

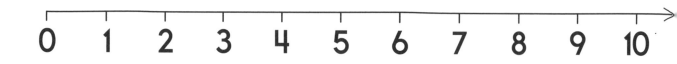

0   1   2   3   4   5   6   7   8   9   10

Now, show the number of children.

0   1   2   3   4   5   6   7   8   9   10

© Disney

On this number line, show how many rocks are in the pile.

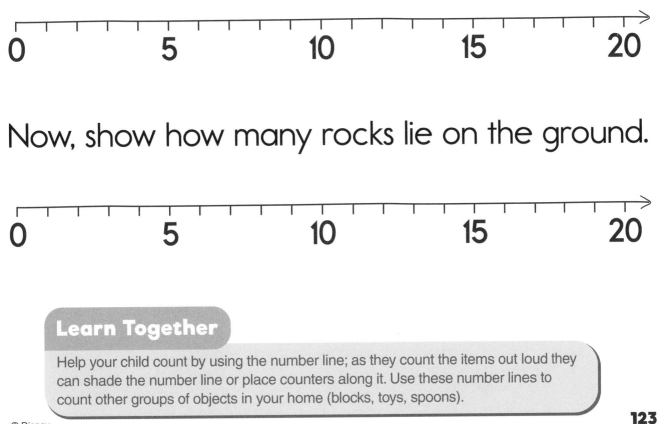

Now, show how many rocks lie on the ground.

Learn Together

Help your child count by using the number line; as they count the items out loud they can shade the number line or place counters along it. Use these number lines to count other groups of objects in your home (blocks, toys, spoons).

© Disney

How Many?

Many things on the island are important to Moana.

Count the objects in each group.

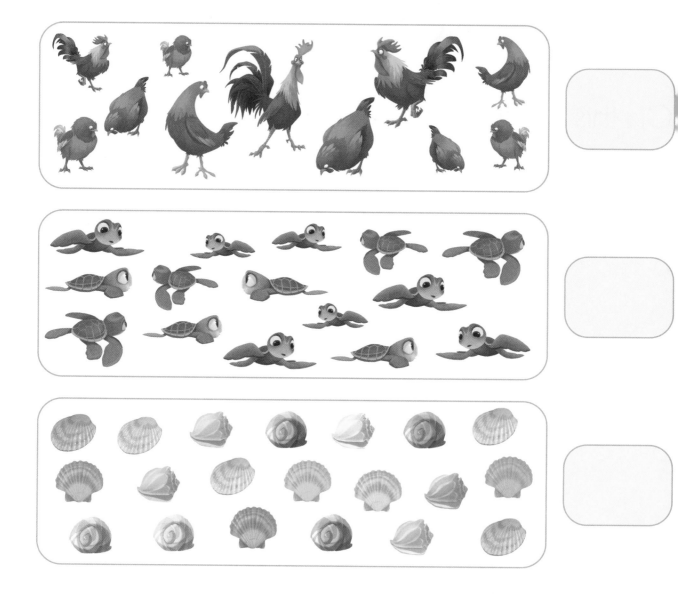

© Disney

Trace each number below.

Draw that number of objects in the box.

14

17

12

Learn Together

With your child, collect groups of **11** to **20** objects (buttons, crayons, toy cars). Ask, "How many do you have?"

© Disney

Count Them All!

Belle's father, Maurice, needs a lot of equipment to make inventions.

Count the objects in each group.

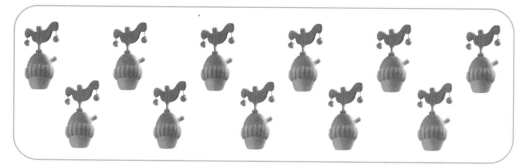

© Disney

On the left, draw 15 objects that Maurice could use in his inventions.

Draw more objects on the right to make 20.

Learn Together

Ask your child to collect **20** small objects (coins, buttons, beads) in a jar. Take turns choosing a number between **11** and **20** and counting that many objects out of and back into the jar.

© Disney

More or Fewer

Abu always wants more!

Write >, <, or = to compare groups.

> more   < fewer   = equal

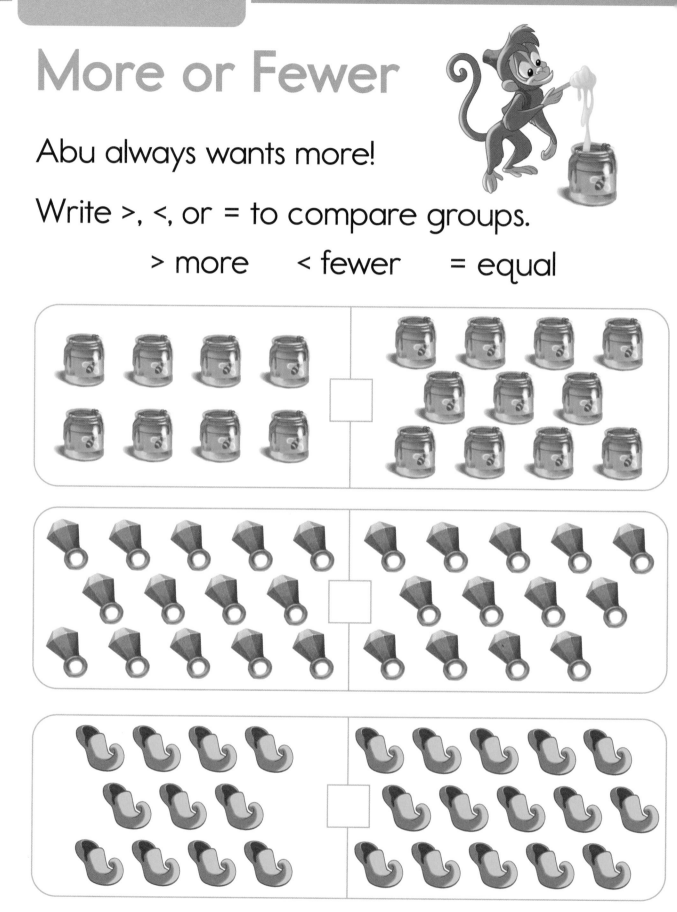

128

© Disney

Here are more of Abu's collections!

Count the objects in each group.

Write >, <, or = to compare groups.

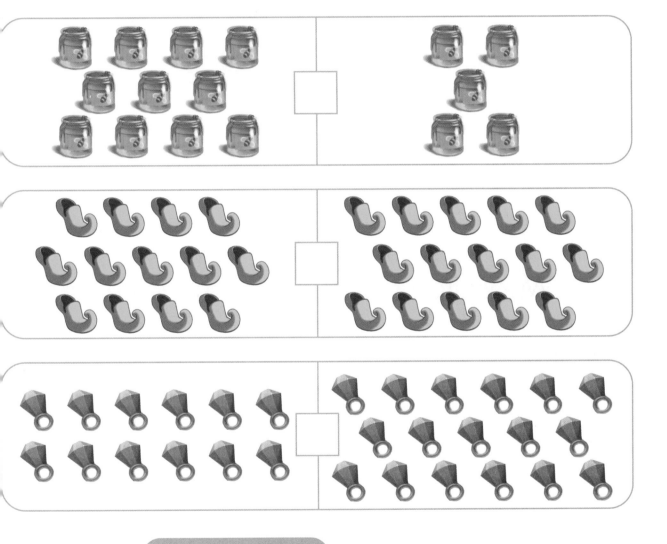

© Disney

Learn Together

Divide **100** small objects into two groups. Your child can count each group and say which has more objects. Which has fewer objects?

What's Missing?

1   2   3   20   7   18
5   16   12
15   6   4
9   8   14
11   17   10
13   19

Duke Weaselton has stolen some numbers!

Can you fill in the missing numbers?

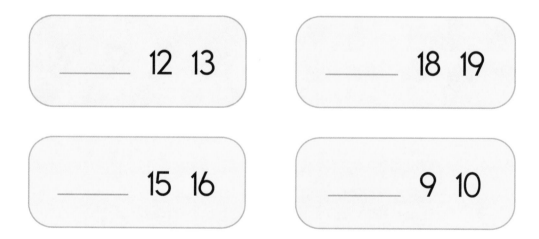

_____ 12 13   _____ 18 19

_____ 15 16   _____ 9 10

© Disney

12 13 _____

15 16 _____

18 19 _____

13 14 _____

16 17 _____

9 10 _____

11 12 _____

17 18 _____

7 8 _____

10 11 _____

14 15 _____

8 9 _____

Learn Together

Using **100** objects, make a group (27 crayons or 38 grapes). Your child can count them out loud. Add 1 more and ask how many there are now.

© Disney

I Think There Are...

Sometimes, you can guess, or estimate, how many objects you see.

Estimate the number of coconuts.

Estimated   Counted

Estimated   Counted

Estimated   Counted

Now, count the coconuts.

© Disney

Estimate the number of cubes.

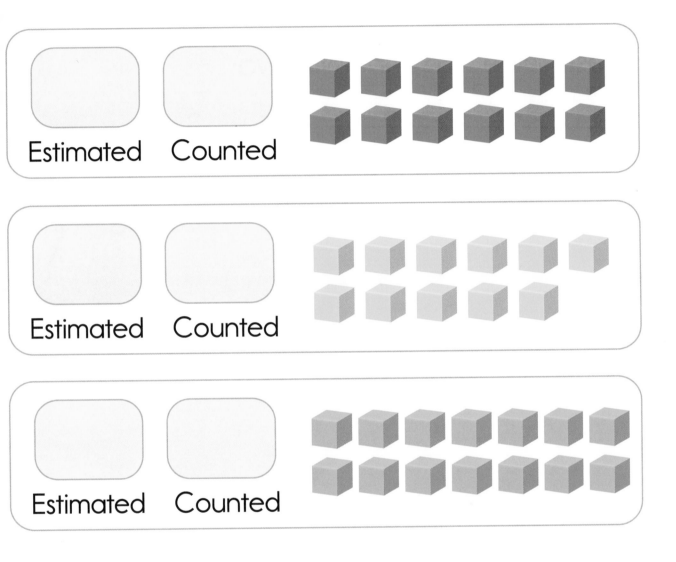

Estimated   Counted

Estimated   Counted

Estimated   Counted

Now, count the cubes.

Learn Together

Help your child understand that they are **estimating** the number before they count. Say, "I think there are 10 coconuts. Let's count! Oh, there are actually 8." Make it clear that it is fine, when estimating, to get an incorrect answer.

© Disney

First, Second, Third

These mice are running away.

Put 1 ✖ under the first mouse.

Put 2 ✖ under the second mouse.

Put 3 ✖ under the third mouse.

Another way to write first is 1st. Another way to write second is 2nd. Another way to write third is 3rd.

© Disney

Put 4 ✖ under the fourth banker.

Put 5 ✖ under the fifth banker.

Put 6 ✖ under the sixth banker.

Another way to write fourth is 4th. Another way to write fifth is 5th. Another way to write sixth is 6th.

Learn Together

Ordinal numbers may be new to your child. Use a calendar to demonstrate the use of ordinal numbers to your child. ("Today is the first day of the week," and so on.)

© Disney

20 to 30

Trace the numbers.

20 20 20 20

21 21 21 21 21

22 22 22 22

23 23 23 23

24 24 24 24

25 25 25 25

© Disney

Trace the numbers.

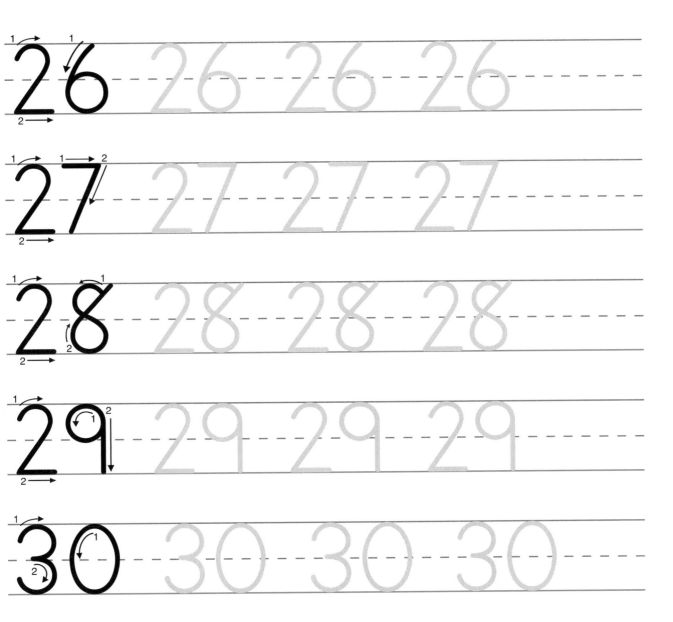

© Disney

Learn Together

Quiz your child with numbers to 120. Give them a number. Ask them to write the numeral and number word.

Show Me the Money

Mr. Big always wants more money!

Draw a line from each coin or bill to how much it is worth.

The first one has been done for you.

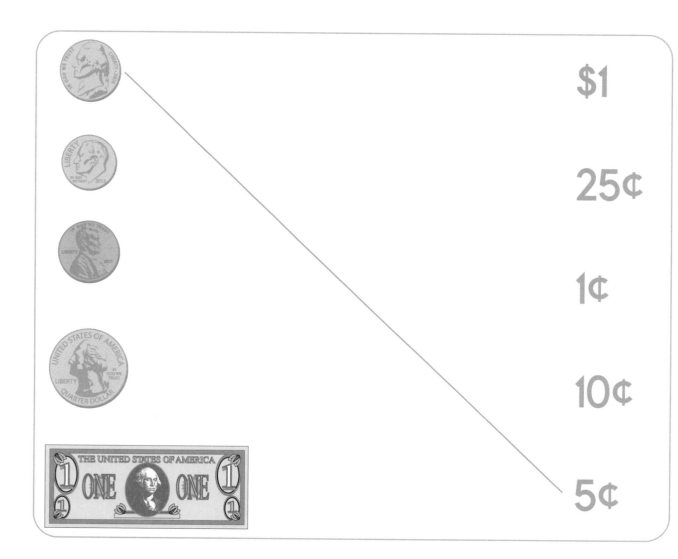

$1

25¢

1¢

10¢

5¢

© Disney

Show 5¢.

Show 10¢ in two different ways.

Show 20¢ in two different ways.

Learn Together

Play "Store" with your child using real money and price tags for some small toys. Take turns shopping and paying.

© Disney

Sort It Out!

Moana sees many
fish when she swims.

(Circle) all the fish with yellow fins.

Underline all the fish without yellow fins.

© Disney

Draw something that belongs in each group.

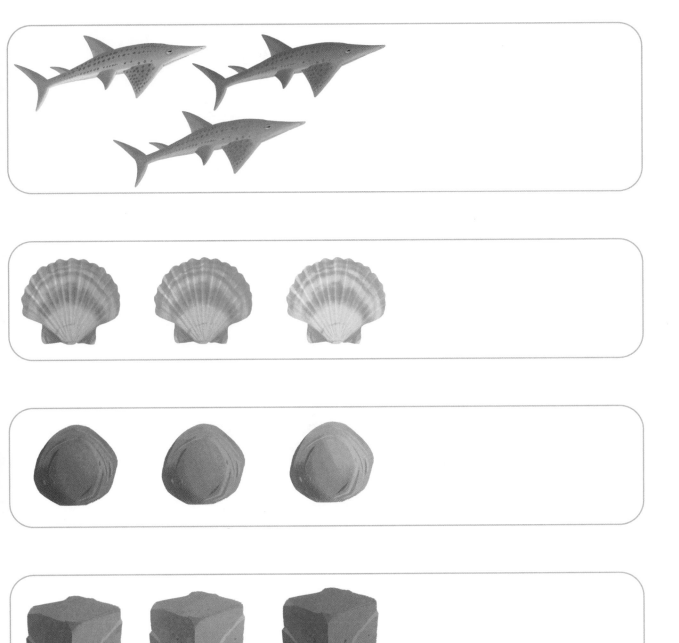

© Disney

Learn Together

Put a variety of socks on a table. Ask your child to help you decide how to sort them (by color, size, or material).

What's the Pattern?

In the Cave of Wonders, Aladdin sees objects arranged in patterns.

What comes next in each pattern?

© Disney

What comes next in each pattern?

X Y X Y X _____

C C T C C _____

1 2 2 1 2 2 1 2 _____

3 3 4 3 3 4 3 _____

ABA ABA ABA _____

Learn Together

Talk about the patterns on these pages, describing each one. Your child can create a pattern using small items around your home (buttons, stickers). Ask your child to describe the pattern.

© Disney

Making Patterns

Mrs. Potts's base has a pattern.

Color the objects below to complete the pattern.

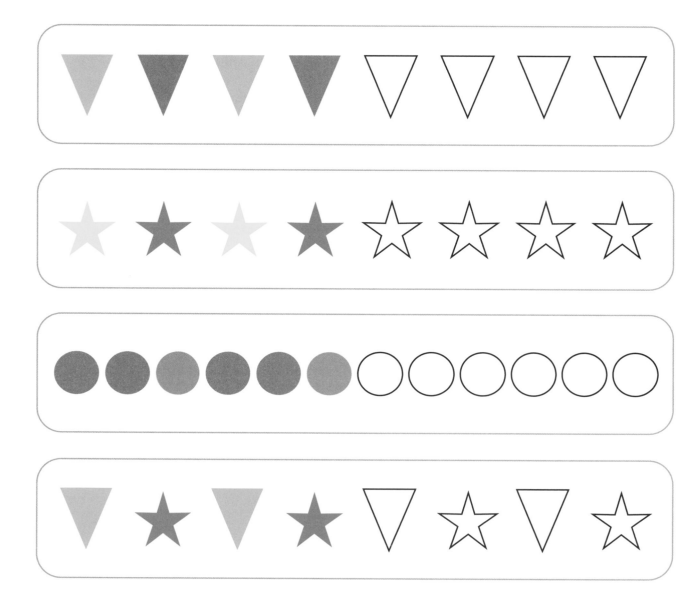

© Disney

Colorful Madame de la Grande Bouche loves patterns.

Choose 2 colors to make a pattern.

Choose 3 colors to make a pattern.

Learn Together

Talk about the patterns on these pages, describing each one. With your child, use small toy animals (or other toys) to make a pattern (horse, pig, horse, pig, horse, pig). Discuss the pattern's rules with your child (color, size, animal type).

© Disney

What's the Sum?

Help Pua gather flowers for Moana.

How many flowers will Pua find?

$$2 \quad + \quad 2 \quad = \quad 4$$

$2 + 2 = 4$ can also be written this way:

$1 + 3 = 4$

© Disney

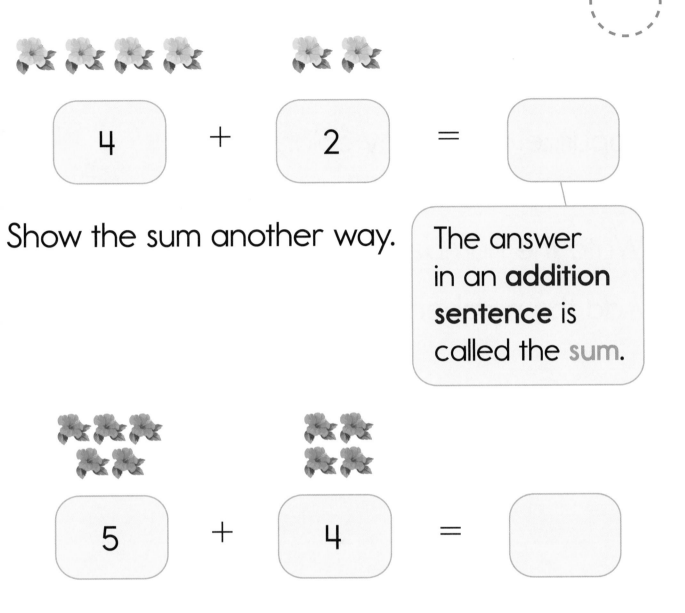

4 + 2 =

Show the sum another way.

The answer in an **addition sentence** is called the sum.

5 + 4 =

Show the sum another way.

Learn Together

Help your child understand that addition involves joining groups, and that there is more than one way to show each of the sums above.

© Disney

Count and Add

Rapunzel uses many colors when she paints.

Write the number in each group.

Add the numbers together.

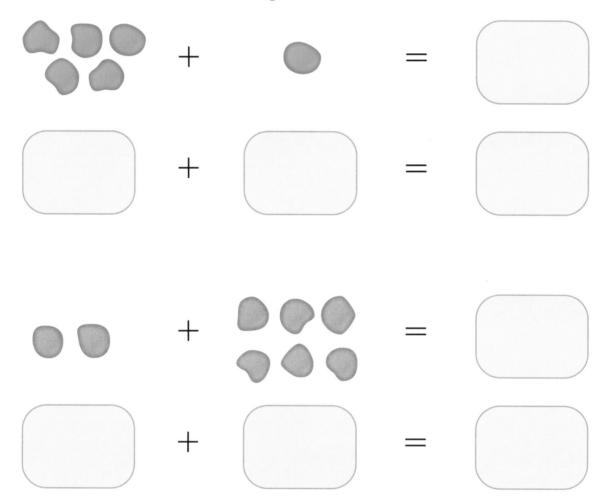

© Disney

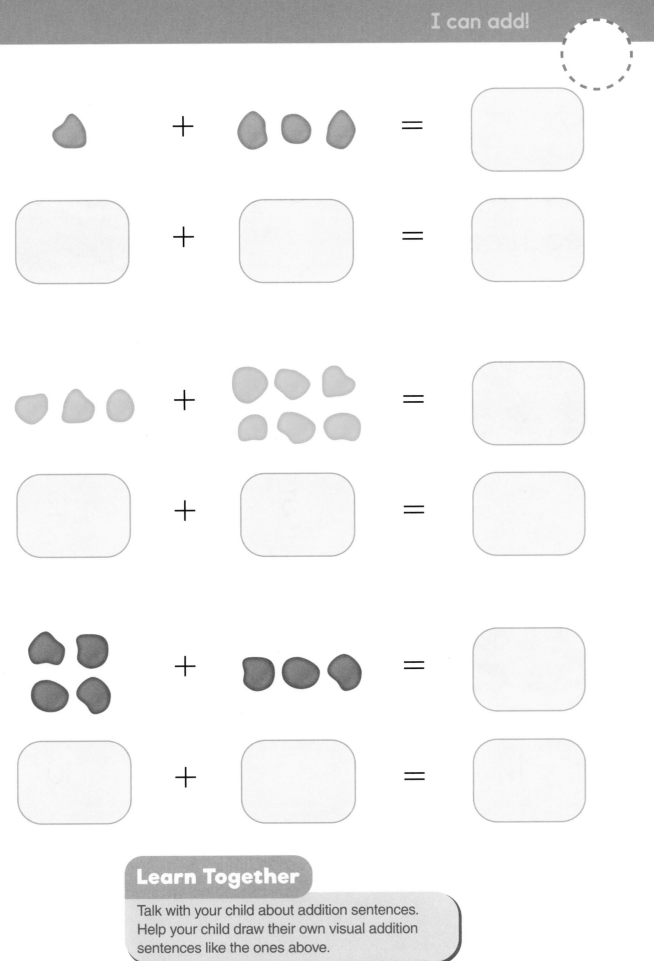

Learn Together

Talk with your child about addition sentences. Help your child draw their own visual addition sentences like the ones above.

© Disney

Solve It

Write the missing numbers in each equation.

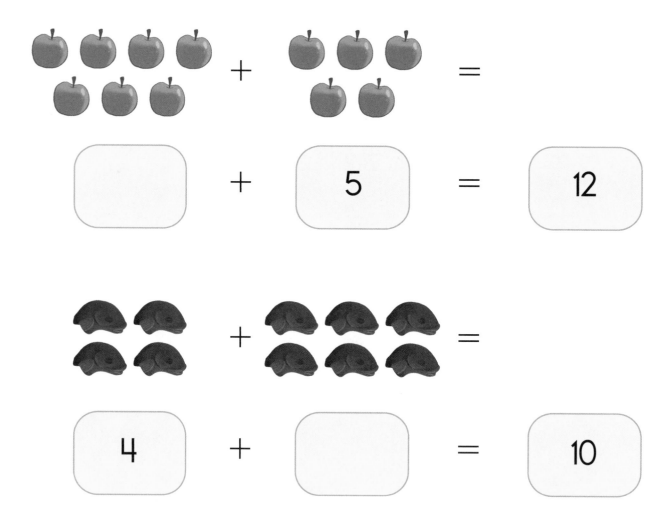

☐ + 5 = 12

4 + ☐ = 10

© Disney

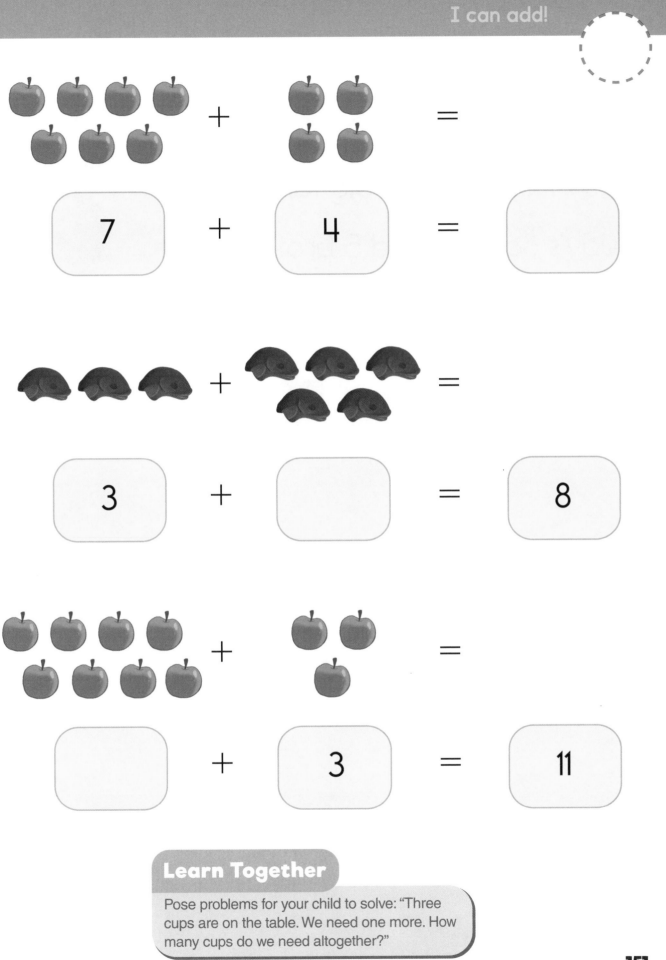

7 + 4 =

3 + ☐ = 8

☐ + 3 = 11

Learn Together

Pose problems for your child to solve: "Three cups are on the table. We need one more. How many cups do we need altogether?"

© Disney

Add Them Up

Judy Hopps has a big family.

Judy's parents and 5 brothers visit her in Zootopia.

Show 2 + 5 on this **10-frame**.

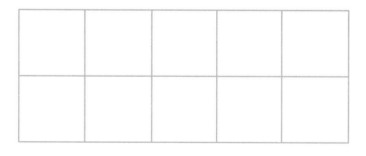

Show the sum another way.

© Disney

Judy's parents and 7 sisters visit her in Zootopia.

+ [ ] =

[ ] + [ ] = [ ]

Show 2 + 7 on this 10-frame.

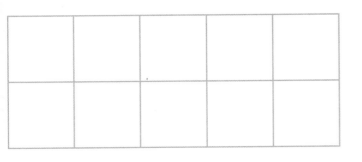

Show the sum another way.

Learn Together

With your child, you can make your own 10-frames. These help children to interpret, build, and write addition (and subtraction) sentences. Work with numbers 11 to 19.

© Disney

Keep Adding

You can add 3 numbers.

Maui's necklace started with 7 shark teeth. He added 3 more. Now, he's going to add 2 more teeth.

$$7 + 3 + 2 = 12$$

© Disney

Solve the 3-number problems.

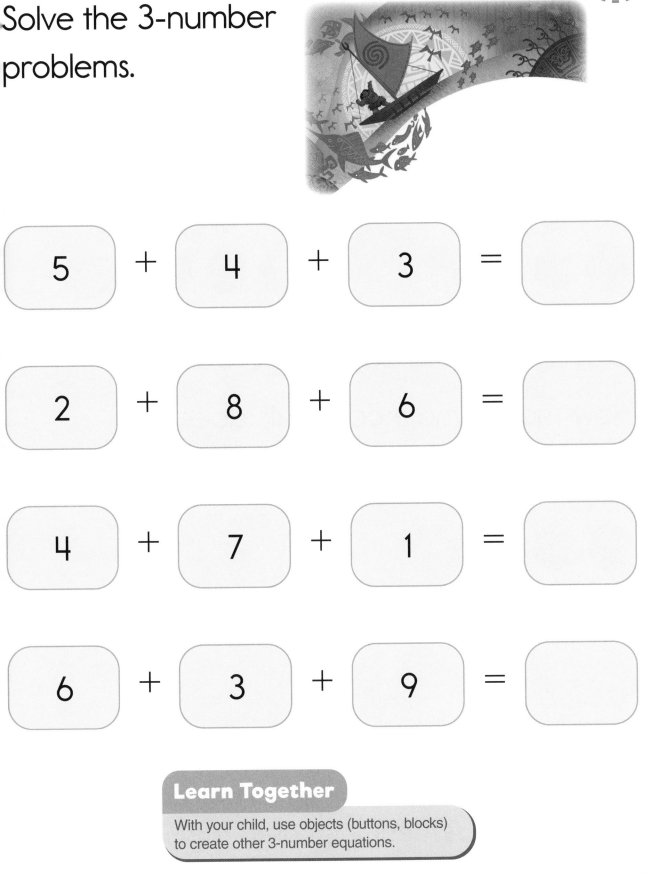

5 + 4 + 3 =

2 + 8 + 6 =

4 + 7 + 1 =

6 + 3 + 9 =

Learn Together

With your child, use objects (buttons, blocks)
to create other 3-number equations.

© Disney

Take It Away

Before

After

One of Moana's coconuts breaks.

How many whole coconuts does Moana have?

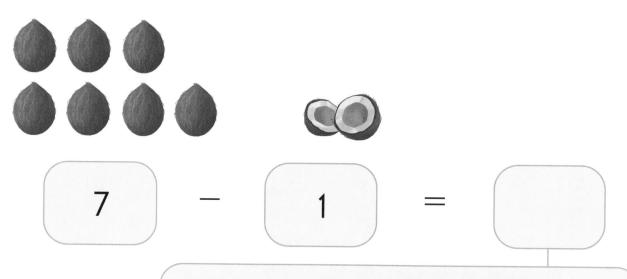

| 7 | − | 1 | = | |

The answer in a **subtraction sentence** is called the difference.

© Disney

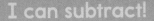

Before

After

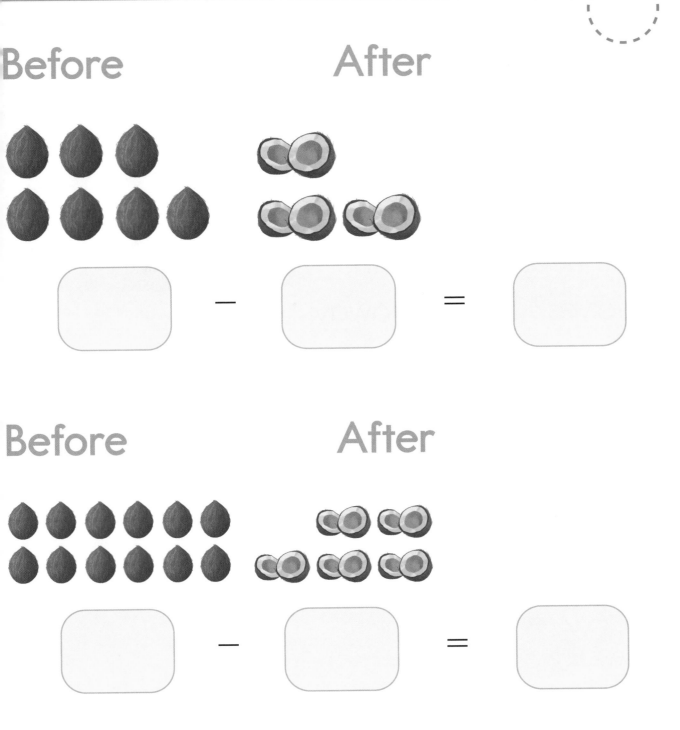

Before

After

Learn Together

Help your child understand subtraction by using objects (buttons, coins, blocks). Count the objects before and after taking some away from a group. You might also create a number line to help them subtract.

© Disney

Take Away Some More

What happens when the Beast roars at the wolves? They run away!

Find the difference.

Use the 10-frames or number line to help you.

$4 - 1 =$ ☐

$5 - 2 =$ ☐

$5 - 3 =$ ☐

$9 - 7 =$ ☐

© Disney

12 − 2 =

17 − 2 =

18 − 8 =

20 − 10 =

0   5   10   15   20

Learn Together

Put 10 objects (coins, paper clips) on a table. Your child can turn away as you cover some of them. Ask your child to identify how many objects are missing and how many are left. Create **number stories** and subtraction sentences together.

© Disney

How Many Are Left?

Write the missing numbers in each equation.

| 9 | − | | = | 7 |

| | − | 4 | = | 6 |

© Disney

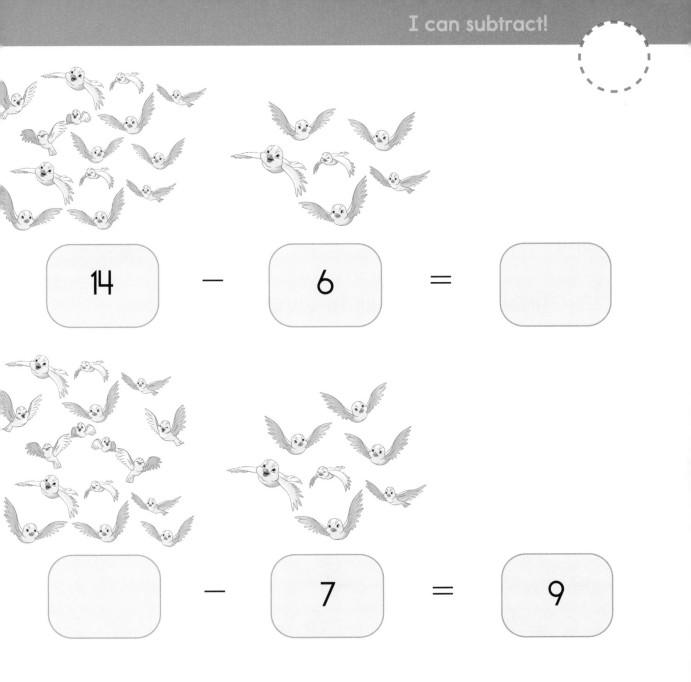

14 – 6 =

☐ – 7 = 9

You can use a number line to help you.

0   5   10   15   20

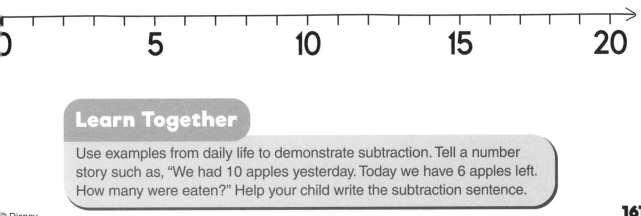

Learn Together

Use examples from daily life to demonstrate subtraction. Tell a number story such as, "We had 10 apples yesterday. Today we have 6 apples left. How many were eaten?" Help your child write the subtraction sentence.

© Disney

What's Left?

Rapunzel has painted every wall in the tower.

Sometimes, she paints over old paintings and starts again.

Count the objects in each group.

Find the difference.

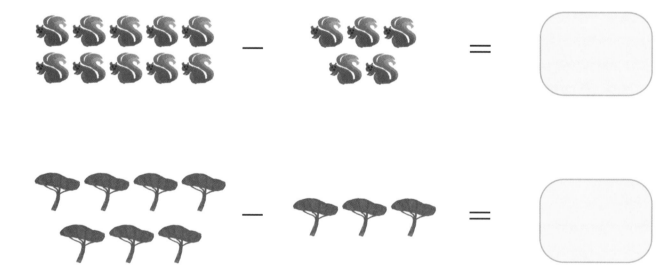

© Disne

Look at the 10-frames.

Write the number in each 10-frame in a blank box.

Find the difference.

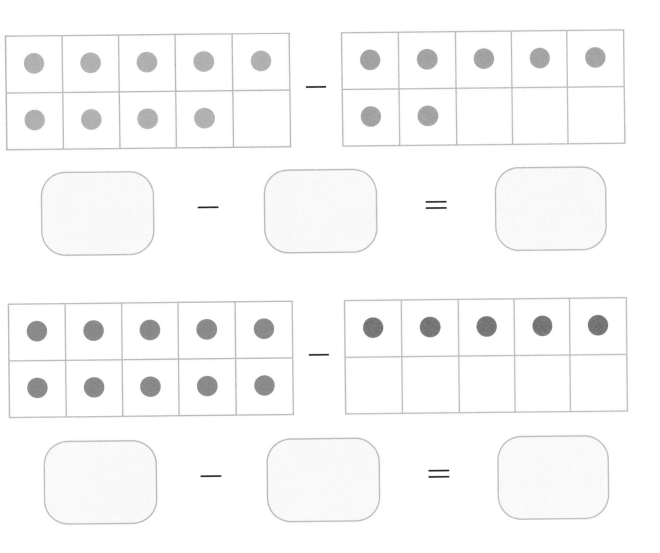

Learn Together

Rather than drawing 10-frames, your child could use connecting blocks in groups of 10. Your child can create number stories for subtraction, disconnecting the indicated number of blocks.

© Disney

Who's Lying?

Nick is trying to figure out if these equations are telling the truth. Help him by writing true by the equations that are correct and false by the equations that are wrong.

10 + 9 = 20 _____

15 – 6 = 9 _____

8 – 7 = 1 _____

13 + 3 = 16 _____

20 – 10 = 0 _____

© Disney

All the equations are lying! Help Nick by changing a number in each to make it true.

$20 + 5 = 24$

$18 - 9 = 8$

$16 - 4 = 12$

$10 - 2 = 7$

$3 + 19 = 23$

$14 + 8 = 20$

$4 + 9 = 12$

$15 - 5 = 5$

Learn Together

Ask your child to come up with their own wrong equation. Then, have them come up with three different ways to make the equation true.

© Disney

Add and Subtract

Tell an addition number story about this picture.

Write an addition sentence about your number story.

Tell a subtraction number story about the picture.

Write a subtraction sentence about your number story.

© Disney

Solve these addition and subtraction sentences.

Use the 10-frames to help you.

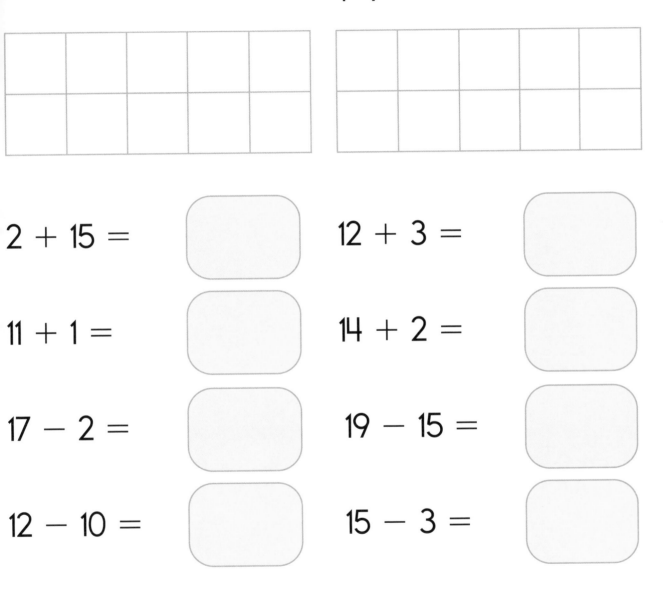

$2 + 15 =$

$11 + 1 =$

$17 - 2 =$

$12 - 10 =$

$12 + 3 =$

$14 + 2 =$

$19 - 15 =$

$15 - 3 =$

Learn Together

Create 9 ten-frames. Work with your child to help them understand that 7 tens = 70, 9 tens = 90, and so on.

© Disney

Add within 100

Moana needs help adding the coconuts being collected in Motunui. Solve the addition problems to help her!

$$\begin{array}{r} 26 \\ +\ 6 \\ \hline \end{array}$$ $$\begin{array}{r} 14 \\ +\ 8 \\ \hline \end{array}$$ $$\begin{array}{r} 32 \\ +\ 2 \\ \hline \end{array}$$

$$\begin{array}{r} 11 \\ +\ 9 \\ \hline \end{array}$$ $$\begin{array}{r} 80 \\ +\ 5 \\ \hline \end{array}$$ $$\begin{array}{r} 51 \\ +\ 4 \\ \hline \end{array}$$

$$\begin{array}{r} 43 \\ +\ 3 \\ \hline \end{array}$$ $$\begin{array}{r} 68 \\ +\ 6 \\ \hline \end{array}$$ $$\begin{array}{r} 77 \\ +\ 1 \\ \hline \end{array}$$

© Disney

The voyagers just brought back the fish they caught. Help Moana add them up!

$$65 + 10$$

$$14 + 20$$

$$47 + 10$$

$$82 + 10$$

$$26 + 30$$

$$53 + 20$$

$$31 + 30$$

$$48 + 10$$

$$79 + 10$$

Learn Together

Help your child with the two-digit addition problems. Have them practice two-digit addition further by asking them to find 10 more than a number or by writing more addition problems for them to solve.

© Disney

Subtract

Duke Weaselton has been busy! He needs help subtracting how many movies he's sold so he knows how many he has left.

$$\begin{array}{r} 60 \\ -10 \\ \hline \end{array} \qquad \begin{array}{r} 30 \\ -10 \\ \hline \end{array} \qquad \begin{array}{r} 40 \\ -10 \\ \hline \end{array}$$

$$\begin{array}{r} 70 \\ -10 \\ \hline \end{array} \qquad \begin{array}{r} 50 \\ -10 \\ \hline \end{array} \qquad \begin{array}{r} 10 \\ -10 \\ \hline \end{array}$$

$$\begin{array}{r} 90 \\ -10 \\ \hline \end{array} \qquad \begin{array}{r} 80 \\ -10 \\ \hline \end{array} \qquad \begin{array}{r} 20 \\ -10 \\ \hline \end{array}$$

© Disney

Now help Finnick! Subtract the pawpsicles he's sold from his total number of pawpsicles.

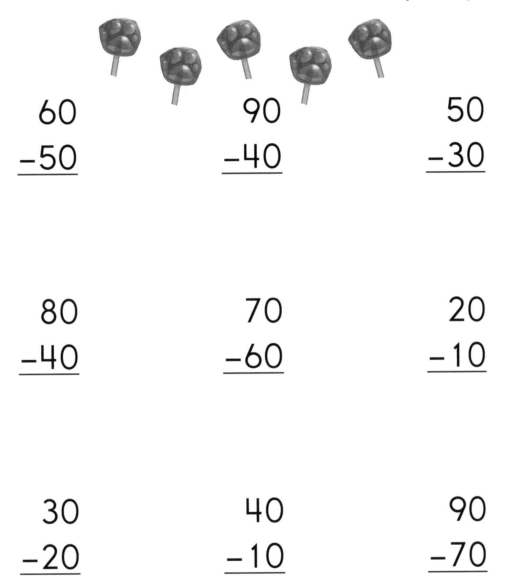

$$60$$
$$-50$$

$$90$$
$$-40$$

$$50$$
$$-30$$

$$80$$
$$-40$$

$$70$$
$$-60$$

$$20$$
$$-10$$

$$30$$
$$-20$$

$$40$$
$$-10$$

$$90$$
$$-70$$

Learn Together

Pose problems for your child to solve using subtraction with multiples of 10: "If Judy gets 40 cases a year and has 20 left to solve, how many cases has she solved so far?"

© Disney

How Long?

These drums come in different sizes.

How many blocks long are these drums?

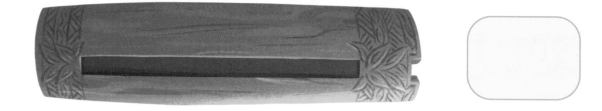

© Disney

How many paper clips long are these objects?

Draw an object that is 7 paper clips long.

Learn Together

Try measuring real objects around your home by using other **non-standard units** (straws, strips of paper of equal lengths, erasers).

© Disney

Which Is Larger?

The Beast is larger than his skates.

One size of each object is missing.

Draw the one that is missing.

Small   Medium   Large

Small   Medium   Large

© Disney

Small

Medium

Large

Small

Medium

Large

Learn Together

Help your child compare the size of various objects around the home. Encourage them to use the words *shorter*, *longer*, *larger*, and *smaller*.

© Disney

How Much Does It Hold?

Abu loves gold.

Which container will hold the most gold?

Circle the container in each row that holds the most.

© Disney

(Circle) the container in each row that holds the least.

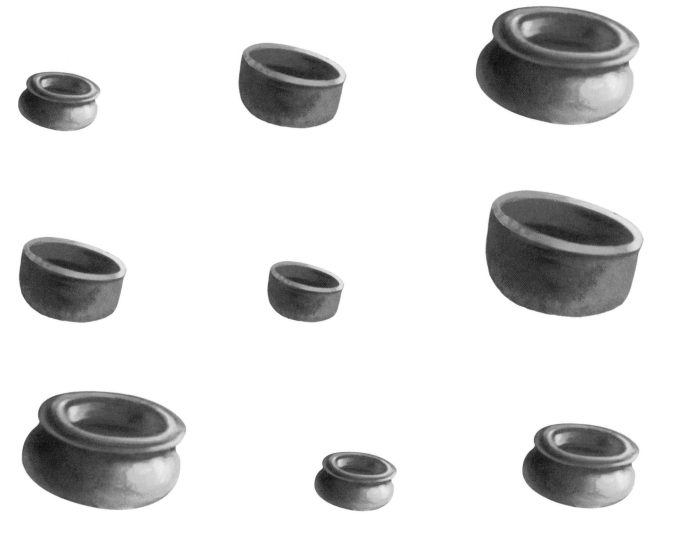

Learn Together

With your child, experiment with water at the sink. Give your child two containers, and ask them to predict which one will hold more. Fill one container with water and then pour it into the other container to see if it overflows.

© Disney

Which Holds More?

Nick is on the hustle, but he needs to figure out which container holds more.

(Circle) the one in each row that holds more.

© Disney

Look at the first photo in each row.

Circle the container that holds less.

© Disney

Learn Together

As you bake or cook, ask your child to help you measure ingredients. Compare the tools you are using. ("Will this cup hold more than this spoon?")

179

Which One Is Heavier?

Which one is heavier?

(Circle) the one that is heavier.

© Disney

Draw something that is light.

Draw something that is heavy.

Learn Together

At home, gather some everyday objects that have very different masses. Your child can hold one item in each hand to determine which one has more mass.

© Disney

Which One Is Lighter?

Pua and Heihei are having fun!

(Circle) the one in each box that is lighter.

© Disney

Draw an object on the left side of the teeter-totter.

Draw something that is lighter on the right side.

Learn Together

Ask your child to explain why they think one object might be lighter than another. Develop a theory that you can investigate together (larger objects are often heavier than smaller objects).

© Disney

What Time Is It?

We can measure time with a clock.

The little hand tells the hour.

The big hand tells the minutes.

Trace the numbers.

This clock reads [ ] o'clock.

© Disney

Add the missing times.

© Disney

Learn Together

Use a real analog clock, or make one from cardboard or a paper plate and craft sticks. Practice telling time with your child. Keep the big hand on the 12 while putting the little hand on different hours.

185

Seeing Circles and Triangles

A circle is a perfectly round shape.

Put an ✖ on one circle in this picture.

Cross out the shapes that are not circles.

© Disney

A triangle has three straight sides.

Put an ✖ on one triangle in this picture.

Cross out the shapes that are not triangles.

Learn Together

Discuss the characteristics of circles and triangles. Ask your child to identify circles and triangles in your home (circular logos on jars, triangular designs on boxes).

© Disney

187

Looking for Rectangles and Squares

A rectangle has four sides.

Two sides are longer than the other two sides.

Circle one rectangle in this picture.

© Disney

A **square** has four equal sides.

Circle one square on Nick's phone.

Write an **R** on the rectangles.

Write an **S** on the squares.

Learn Together

With your child, cut out circles and rectangles. Cut them into 2 and 4 equal shares. Explain halves and fourths.

© Disney

What's That Shape?

A pentagon has five sides.

The Sultan's blue ring is shaped like a pentagon.

Cross out the shapes that are not pentagons.

© Disney

A hexagon has six sides.

Look at the hexagons on this gem.

Write a P on the pentagons below.

Write an H on the hexagons below.

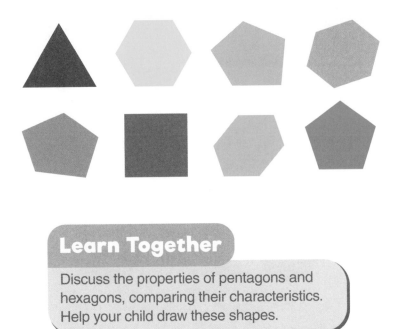

Learn Together

Discuss the properties of pentagons and hexagons, comparing their characteristics. Help your child draw these shapes.

© Disney

Solid Objects

This object is called a sphere.

(Circle) the sphere on the sword.

Cross out the objects that are not spheres.

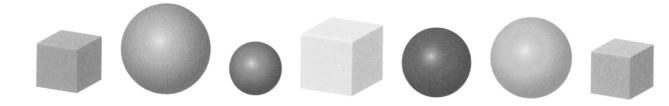

© Disney

This object is called a cube.

Circle a lantern that looks like a cube.

Cross out the objects that are not cubes.

Learn Together

Ask your child to look at the **2-dimensional** and **3-dimensional** shapes from this section. Challenge them to create pictures of animals, vehicles, buildings, and more!

© Disney

More Solid Objects

This object is called a cylinder.

The bottoms of these towers are shaped like cylinders. Circle one of the cylinders.

Cross out the objects that are not cylinders.

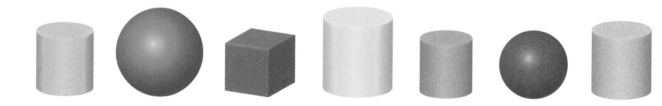

© Disney

This object is called a cone.

Circle the cone in this picture.

Cross out the objects that are not cones.

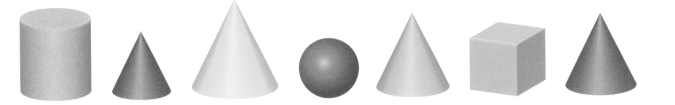

Learn Together

Encourage your child to build with blocks, small boxes, cans, or other items found around the home. Name their shapes.

© Disney

Words for Where

Some words tell us where people or objects are.

Match each resident of Zootopia to the correct word.

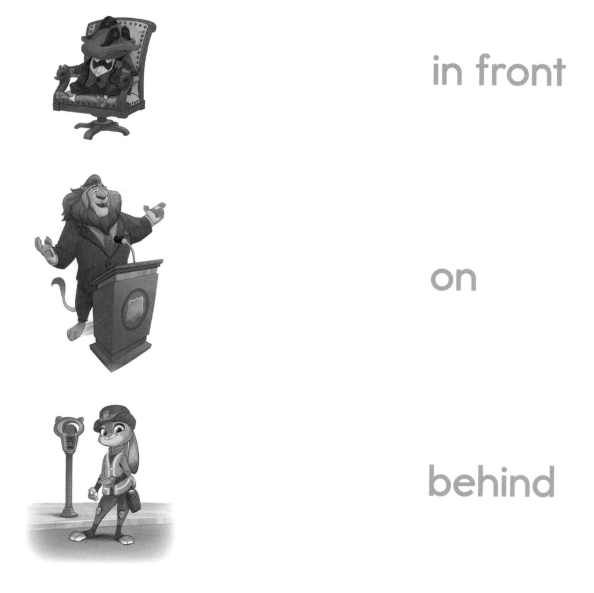

in front

on

behind

© Disney

Look at this picture.

Circle something that is above.

Underline something that is between.

Draw an ✖ on something that is under.

Draw a ✔ on something that is in.

Learn Together

Your child can choose a word (*behind/under*) from these pages and act it out. Take turns acting and guessing.

© Disney

Same or Different?

The Stabbington Brothers look alike in many ways.

But they also look different.

How do they look alike?

_____

_____

How do they look different?

_____

_____

© Disney

Circle the objects in each group that are the same.

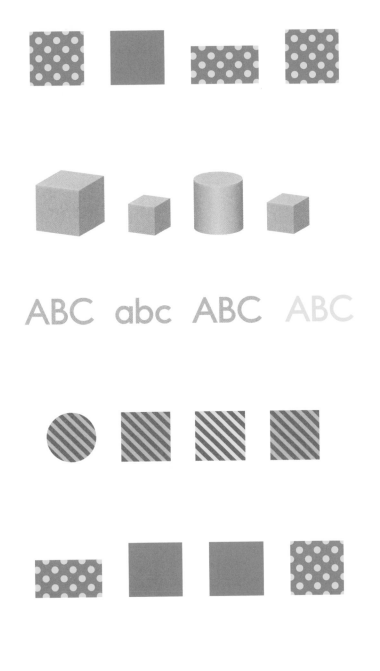

ABC abc ABC ABC

Learn Together

Ask your child to explain the reasoning they used to complete these activities. Play a game of "one of these things is not like the others" using toys. Take turns choosing the group of toys and creating a rule.

© Disney

What Belongs?

Circle the objects in each group that go together.

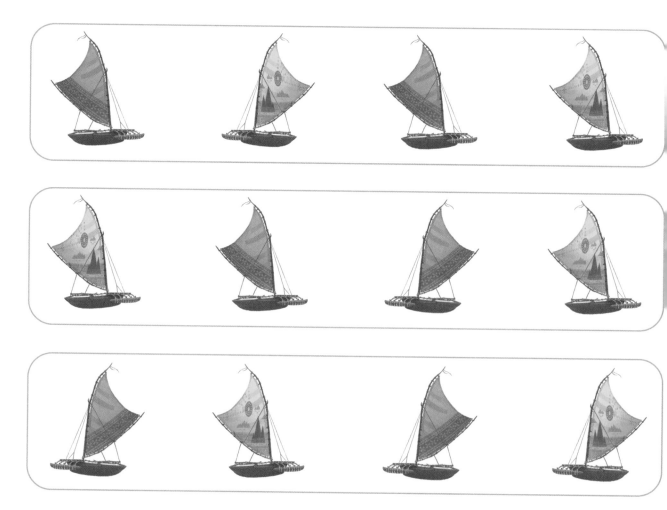

© Disney

Look at the first picture in each row.

Circle the other picture that is the same.

Learn Together

Your child can collect 15 small objects and sort them by color, shape, or another attribute.

© Disney

Find the Rule!

Cross out the one in each group that does not belong.

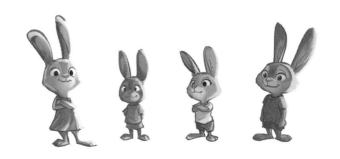

Rule: _____

Rule: _____

© Disney

Look at the first picture in each row.

Decide if it belongs in the group on the right.

Cross it out if it does not belong.

Circle it if it does belong.

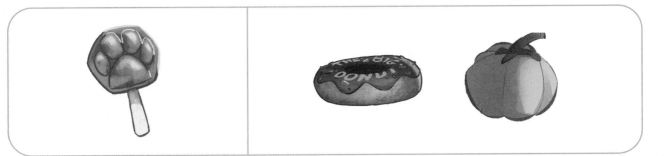

Learn Together

Help your child understand the rule for each category. Put several items (kitchen items, books) together with one item that "does not belong." Ask your child to tell you which item does not belong.

© Disney

Sort It!

Rapunzel's room needs cleaning up.

Put a 1 beside the objects that go in Basket 1.

Put a 2 beside the objects that go in Basket 2.

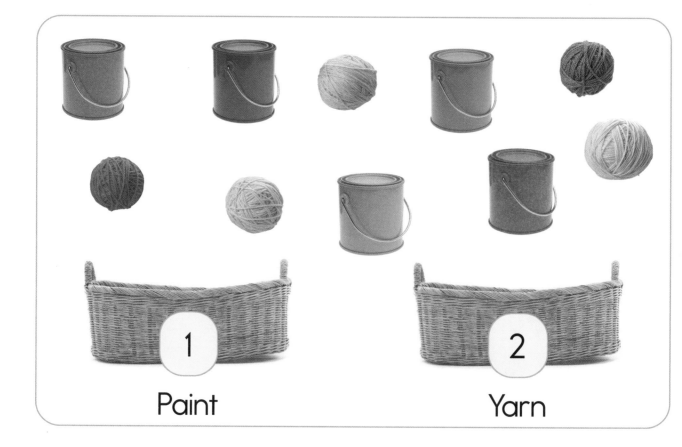

1
Paint

2
Yarn

© Disney

What rule will you use to sort these objects?

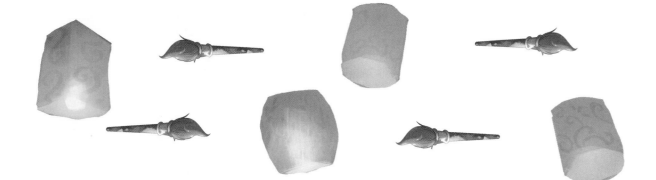

Label the boxes.

Put a 1 beside the objects that go in Box 1.

Put a 2 beside the objects that go in Box 2.

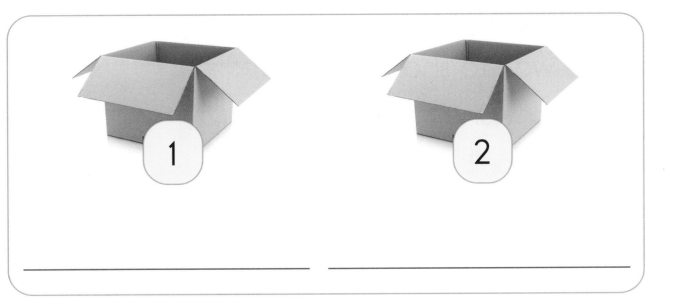

Learn Together

Help your child develop a rule for the sorting activity above, and then help them label the boxes. Discuss how else the items might be sorted (by material, color, or whether or not your child likes them).

© Disney

The Shell Graph

Moana finds some shells.

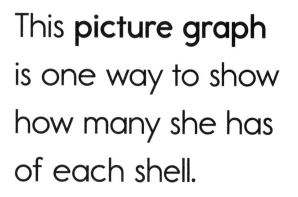

This **picture graph** is one way to show how many she has of each shell.

Moana's Shells

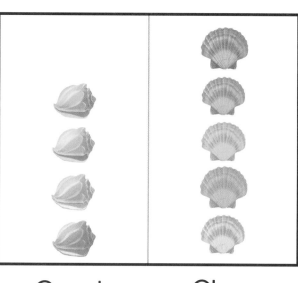

Conch shells   Clam shells

© Disney

Create your own picture graph.

Label your picture graph.

Give it a title.

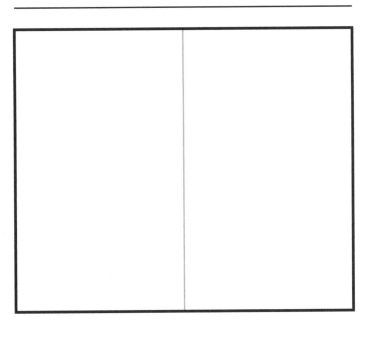

Tell one thing your picture graph shows.

Learn Together

Help your child create their picture graph. To keep it manageable, guide them to choose objects that they don't have too many of and that they can sort into two categories. For example, they could sort their shoes; the sorting rule might be laces or no laces.

© Disney

Show How Many

© Disney

Look at all the yarn Rapunzel has!

Create a picture graph.

Rapunzel's Yarn

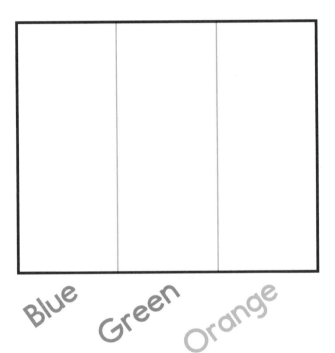

Blue Green Orange

What color yarn does Rapunzel have the most of? _____

What color yarn does Rapunzel have the least of? _____

Learn Together

Ask your child questions about the picture graph.
Example: "If Rapunzel needs five balls of yarn to knit
Flynn a sweater, what color will the sweater be?"

© Disney

Organizing Information

Judy writes a lot of tickets!

Each ticket matches a license plate.

© Disney

Create a picture graph.

License Plates

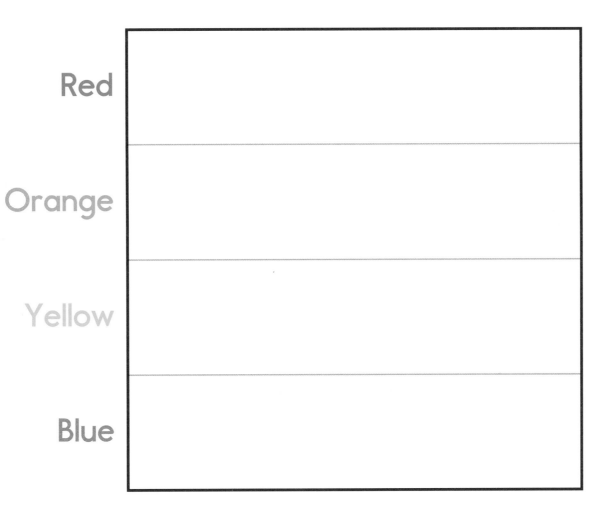

Red

Orange

Yellow

Blue

Tell two things your picture graph shows.

Learn Together

When discussing graphs, encourage your child to use comparative language (*more, fewer, most, fewest*). Ask, "What color plate is there the most of? The fewest of?"

© Disney

Language Arts

As your child completes the lessons in this book, extend their learning with some of the following activities.

Letters and Sounds

- Read alphabet books together. Encourage your child to suggest other words that begin with each letter.

- Serve a bowl of alphabet soup or cereal. Challenge your child to identify every letter and then connect each letter to an object in your home (*c* is for *couch*).

- Every week, choose a new letter or pair of letters to be "super" letters. Print the letter extra big, and place it where your child can see it. Challenge your child to find as many objects as possible that begin with that letter or letter pair.

- Help your child create a dance or song for each letter of the alphabet.

- Stamp out letter shapes in the snow or sand.

- Give your child various materials (pencils, crayons, markers, clay, beads, sand, chalk, paper, magnet letters) that they can use to make letters and words.

- Give your child index cards to create phonics flash cards. Help them choose word families, blends, and digraphs to practice.

Word Knowledge

- Ask your child to help you create a grocery list.

- Your child can read familiar words on boxes and cans of food.

- Your child can read signs in your neighborhood.

- Pause as you read to your child, allowing them to read sight words or other words they know.

© Disney

Comprehension

- Invite your child to tell you stories about their day.

- Encourage your child to make connections to stories they read and shows they watch.

- Tell stories together. Get your child to finish a familiar story.

- Your child can retell simple or familiar stories they have heard; this is an important step in understanding how stories are structured.

- As you read or watch shows, ask your child questions to help them make predictions. ("Aladdin found a magic lamp. What do you think he'll do next?")

- Encourage your child's questions about stories and nonfiction text.

- Point to the pictures in stories. Talk about the characters or setting.

- Tell a familiar story out of sequence and ask your child to fix it.

- Talk about the beginning, middle, and end of stories.

Writing

- Create sentence starters for your child to finish. ("I want a _____." "Do you want to go to the _____?" "I love _____.")

- Create a digital photo album together, with photos of your child's life. Help them write the captions.

- Write stories (lists, letters, poems, texts) with your child.

- Write notes to each other and leave them in secret places.

- Together, create a treasure map for your child to follow.

- Your child can write labels or captions for their drawings.

© Disney

Math

Number Sense

- Count together as you do everyday activities. ("How many toys are we putting away?" "How many blocks does this house need? Let's count!")

- Sing counting songs or skipping rhymes with your child.

- Read counting books together.

- Practice counting by starting at numbers other than one. This sequence is harder for children to remember because it's irregular.

- Make a counting book using your child's toys and digital photos.

- Give your child various materials (pencils, crayons, markers, clay, beads, sand, chalk, paper) that they can use to make numbers and number words.

- Place 1 to 100 small objects, such as dried beans, into a cup. Your child can estimate and then count the number of objects.

- Use 100 small objects to make number groups (20 objects, 42 objects). Your child can write the number and the word for that number.

Patterns

- Invite your child to help you sort as you do chores (putting away dishes, laundry, or toys).

- Look for patterns in your home and neighborhood.

- Take photos of patterns you see. With your child, create a digital pattern book with captions to describe each pattern.

- Use stickers or toys to create patterns for each other to complete.

© Disney

Addition and Subtraction

- Add or subtract as you do everyday activities together. ("How many more apples do we need in the bag to make 10?" "We have too many carrots for the stew. We only need 5. How many should we take away?")

- Play card and board games that involve adding or subtracting.

- Create clues for a scavenger hunt that can be solved only by addition or subtraction. ("You need to find 8 toys in your room and 3 toys in the living room. How many toys will you have then? That answer will tell you how many steps to take from the bathroom to your room to find the next clue.")

Measurement

- Read and follow recipes together. Allow your child to measure ingredients and identify how much of something is needed. ("This soup needs 3 onions and 1 carrot.")

- Count the squares in the sidewalk as you walk in your neighborhood. How many squares is your home from the park?

- Experiment with the mass and capacity of everyday objects. ("Do you think this book is heavier than this pencil? Why do you think that? Let's lift them both to find out." "Do you think this cup will hold more water than this bowl? How can we find out?")

© Disney

Bonus Activities

Geometry

- Look for 3-D objects in your home, noting which objects are which shapes (cans are cylinders). Your child can use a notebook to draw and label the objects and shapes they found. Then, use the objects you found to build a town.

- Look for shapes as you walk in your neighborhood. ("That door is a rectangle. The window is a square.")

- Take photos of the shapes you see and create a shapes photo album.

Collecting and Using Data

- Encourage your child to sort objects, such as toys, by providing them with bins or other containers. Talk about the rules they use to sort. ("All of the red toys went in the red bin. Are you sorting by color?")

- Help your child develop a survey for family members to complete. ("What movie should we watch tonight?" "What toppings should we have on our pizza?") Work together to graph the results.

- Look for graphs, tables, and charts as you read nonfiction. Help your child understand the information in these texts.

© Disney

Glossary

2-dimensional: something that has length and width but no depth. Shapes that are 2-dimensional include circles, squares, and triangles.

3-dimensional: something that has length, width, and depth. Shapes that are 3-dimensional include spheres, cubes, and cylinders.

10-frames: two-by-five rectangle frames into which counters are placed to illustrate numbers less than or equal to 10. These frames help teach counting and can help your child with addition and subtraction.

addition sentences: number sentences or equations used to express addition. For example, 4 + 1 = 5.

adjectives: words that describe nouns.

alphabetical order: to arrange words according to the order of letters in the alphabet; your child is at a stage where they can arrange some words in alphabetical order by first letter only (that is, *bread*, *clock*, *dog*, but not *brake*, *bread*, *break*).

base word: the most basic form of a word, without any affixes.

blends: two or more consonants that work together in a word, but each consonant can be distinctly heard. For example, the *sn* in *snake* or the *ft* in *raft*.

common nouns: nouns that name general people, places, or things. Some common nouns are *dogs*, *tree*, *girl*, *park*.

contraction: words created by joining two words and using an apostrophe to replace the missing letters (*don't*, *I'm*, *you're*). Your child is ready to read simple and common contractions but will have greater difficulty with uncommon ones and may not be ready to spell or write any contractions.

digraphs: two consonants working together to make one sound. For example, the *sh* in *shake* or the *ck* in *block*.

estimating: to use understanding of numbers to make an educated guess at an answer to a problem. At this stage, your child is ready to estimate how many objects are in a group of 10.

fiction: writing that was invented by the imagination and does not tell about actual events; fiction texts include novels, storybooks, fairy tales, and some poems.

homophones: words that sound the same but are spelled differently (*your/you're*, *to/two/too*). Your child may recognize a few common homophones as they read but may still use the wrong homophone when writing.

key details: the information in a text that helps the understanding of the main idea of the text. These details might answer the questions *who, what, when, where,* and *why*.

© Disney

letter combinations: two or more letters working together in a word. Letter combinations include blends and digraphs.

long vowel sound: the sound a vowel makes depends on the letters around it and its position in the word. An example of a long vowel sound is the sound *a* makes in *cake* (as opposed to the short vowel sound of the *a* in *cat*).

make connections: a reading strategy that supports your child's understanding of texts. There are three types of connections (text to self, text to text, and text to world). At this stage of development, your child will mostly be making text-to-self connections; that is, as they listen to you read, they will make connections to those things they have experienced or feelings they have had. Meaningful connections can help them understand what a character is feeling or what has happened in the text.

nonfiction text: writing based in truth or reality; nonfiction texts include posters, instructions, diagrams, diaries, some magazine and newspaper articles, blogs, and so on. Your child is beginning to identify the differences between fiction and nonfiction.

non-standard units: units for measuring that are not conventional. So, for example, your child might measure two books by using an eraser ("This book is 6 erasers long. That book is 8 erasers long."). While your child may not be ready to understand centimeters, liters, kilograms, etc., they can use non-standard units to measure.

number line: a line showing numbers placed in order. Number lines can help your child as they add or subtract or think about how one number is related to another (3 comes before 6, 10 is 9 numbers away from 1).

number stories: one or more statements that illustrate math equations. For example, the equation $2 + 2 = 4$ could be told as a story about two children who are joined by two friends.

one-to-one correspondence: in math, the idea that objects in one group correspond to objects in a second group. Understanding this concept helps your child form a sound foundation for understanding math.

ordinal numbers: numbers that express order, such as *first*, *second*, *third*.

picture graph: a graph that uses pictures or symbols to represent objects. Your child will be creating a variety of graphs in school, including vertical and horizontal pictographs, bar graphs, and line plots.

possessive: showing ownership. Nouns and pronouns can be possessive. Examples of words showing possession are *my* book or *Judy's* badge.

© Disney

prefix: an affix that comes at the beginning of a word and changes a word's meaning.

pronoun: a word that takes the place of a noun. Some examples of pronouns are *he, she, it, they, this.*

proper nouns: nouns that name a specific person, place, or thing. Some proper nouns are *Rapunzel, Corona,* and *Pascal.*

rhyming words: words that have the same end sound (*pop, stop, hop*). Your child is ready to identify rhyming words and the part of the word that makes the same sound. As you list rhyming words together, try to focus on those that have the same spelling (*feed* and *seed,* rather than *feed* and *bead*).

short vowel sound: the sound a vowel makes depends on the letters around it and its position in the word. An example of a short vowel sound is the sound *a* makes in *hat* (as opposed to the long vowel sound of the *a* in *hate*).

sight words: short, simple words your child will begin to recognize immediately as they become more familiar with reading. Sight words for children at this level include *a, about, am, an, and, are, as, be, because, big, but, by, did, do, don't, for, from, had, has, have, he, her, here, him, his, how, I, if, I'm, in, into, is, it, just, like, me, mother, my, no, not, now, of, on, one, or, our, out, over, see, she, so, the, their, them, then, there, they, this, to, too, two, up, us, was, we, went, were, what, when, where, who, you, your.*

subtraction sentences: number sentences or equations used to express subtraction. For example, $6 - 2 = 4$.

suffix: an affix that comes at the end of a word and changes a word's meaning.

syllable: a unit of spoken language in a word. A syllable must have at least one vowel. The name Moana has three syllables, *Mo, an, a.* Notice the vowel in each syllable.

verb tense: form of a verb that expresses a time frame — past, present, or future. Past tense verbs tell us about actions or events that happened in the past (I *played* soccer). To make a regular verb past tense, add *ed.* If the verb ends in *e,* just add *d.* Present tense verbs tell us about actions or events happening now (I *play* soccer). Future tense verbs tell us about actions or events that will happen in the future. They are created by adding the helping verb *will* with the base form of a verb (I *will play* soccer).

word family: a group of words related in some way, such as beginning or ending with the same sound (*bed, fed, red* are part of the *ed* word family; *black, blue, blond* are part of the *bl* word family).

© Disney

The Case of the Missing Letters

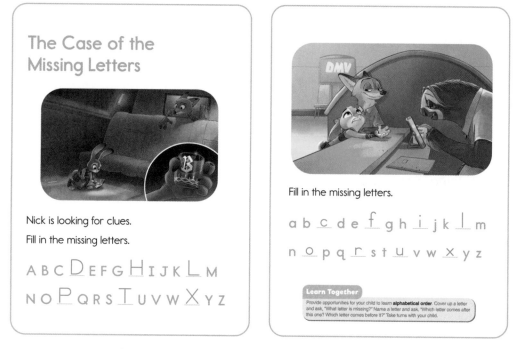

Nick is looking for clues.

Fill in the missing letters.

A B C D E F G H I J K L M
N O P Q R S T U V W X Y Z

22

Fill in the missing letters.

a b c d e f g h i j k l m
n o p q r s t u v w x y z

Learn Together
Provide opportunities for your child to learn **alphabetical order**. Cover up a letter and ask, "What letter is missing?" Name a letter and ask, "Which letter comes after this one? Which letter comes before it?" Take turns with your child.

23

Matching Letters

The letters in the library are a mess.

Match up the letters.

The first one has been done for you.

A — d
D — p
Q — a
P — b
B — q

24

Now, match up these letters.

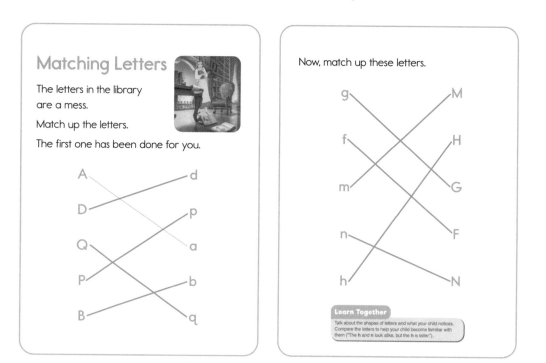

g — M
f — H
m — G
n — F
h — N

Learn Together
Talk about the shapes of letters and what your child notices. Compare the letters to help your child become familiar with them ("The h and n look alike, but the h is taller.").

25

© Disney

Princess Puzzle Time!

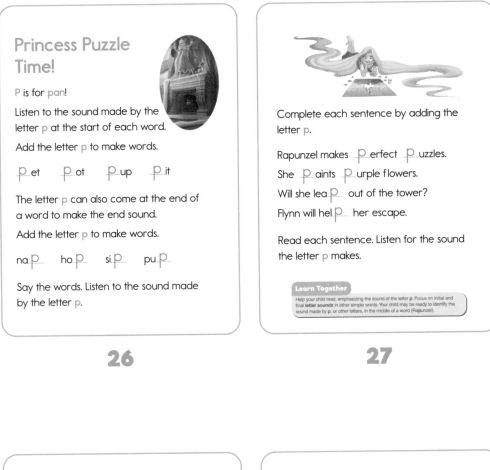

P is for pan!

Listen to the sound made by the letter p at the start of each word.

Add the letter p to make words.

Pet   Pot   Pup   Pit

The letter p can also come at the end of a word to make the end sound.

Add the letter p to make words.

naP   hoP   siP   puP

Say the words. Listen to the sound made by the letter p.

26

Complete each sentence by adding the letter p.

Rapunzel makes Perfect Puzzles.
She Paints Purple flowers.
Will she leaP out of the tower?
Flynn will helP her escape.

Read each sentence. Listen for the sound the letter p makes.

Learn Together
Help your child read, emphasizing the sound of the letter p. Focus on initial and final **letter sounds** in other simple words. Your child may be ready to identify the sound made by p, or other letters, in the middle of a word (Rapunzel).

27

In the Family

You can add p to an to make pan.
Add c, t, v, and m to an to make new words.
Say each word out loud.

can   tan   van   man

These words are all part of the an word family. Can you think of other words that are part of this family? Answers will vary.
Sample answers:

ran   fan   pan

Add letters to make words that belong to the op **word family**.

hop   cop   mop   pop

28

Add letters to make words that belong to the at word family.

hat   rat   sat   pat

Can you think of other words that are part of this family? Answers will vary.
Sample answers:

bat   cat   mat

Add letters to make words that belong to the ug word family.

hug   bug   mug   rug

Learn Together
Help your child read these words, emphasizing their sounds. Use the words to make silly sentences (Hug the bug on the rug.). Make other words with these and other word families.

29

© Disney

More Words, Please!

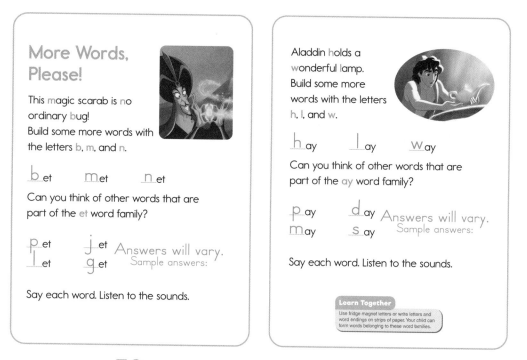

This magic scarab is no ordinary bug!
Build some more words with the letters b, m, and n.

b_et   m_et   n_et

Can you think of other words that are part of the et word family?

p_et   j_et
l_et   g_et

Answers will vary.
Sample answers:

Say each word. Listen to the sounds.

30

Aladdin holds a wonderful lamp.
Build some more words with the letters h, l, and w.

h_ay   l_ay   w_ay

Can you think of other words that are part of the ay word family?

p_ay   d_ay
m_ay   s_ay

Answers will vary.
Sample answers:

Say each word. Listen to the sounds.

Learn Together
Use fridge magnet letters or write letters and word endings on strips of paper. Your child can form words belonging to these word families.

31

Working Together

Judy and Nick learn to work together. Some letters work together too. For example, the b and l in blue work together. Say the word. Listen to the sound bl makes at the beginning of the word.

Build some words using letters that work together. Answers will vary.
Sample answers:

sl   bl   fl

bl_ock   sl_ow   sl_eep
fl_op   sl_ip   fl_aw

Say each word you made.

32

Nick and Judy help each other to the very end.
Some letters help each other to create a single sound.

Build some words using letters that work together. Answers will vary.
Sample answers:

ch   sh   th   wh

ch_air   fi_sh   wh_ale
ba_th   ch_ild   wi_th

Say each word you made.
Make some more words with these sounds.

Learn Together
Help your child work out which of the blends or digraphs to add. If they add the wrong one, say the word with your child, and ask if they think it sounds right. Note that more than one letter combination may work. Experiment with other letter combinations.

33

© Disney

Short and Long

Vowels help you make words. Some vowels make a **short vowel sound**. The a in hat and the u in nut are short vowels.

Add the missing vowels to the sentences below.

Moana holds a special r o ck in her h a nd.

The p i g is in the n e t.

Read the sentences out loud. Listen to the vowel sounds.

34

Sometimes, vowels make a **long vowel sound**. This sound is like their letter names. The o in no is a long vowel.

Underline the vowel in each word that makes the long vowel sound.

w<u>a</u>ke h<u>e</u> l<u>i</u>ke b<u>o</u>ne <u>u</u>se g<u>o</u>ld b<u>e</u> s<u>o</u>

Say each word.

Learn Together
Play "Short or Long?" with your child. List words that have a short vowel sound (cup, rug) or a long vowel sound (bike, home). Take turns saying words. Help your child identify vowel sounds as short or long.

35

Team Work!

Judy and Nick are a team. Like Judy and Nick, sometimes vowels work together as a team. You only hear one sound. Team has a long e sound.

Underline the vowel letters in each word. Write the long vowel sound you hear.

b<u>ee</u>t e   b<u>ea</u>d e   w<u>ai</u>t a
n<u>ee</u>d e   b<u>oa</u>t o   g<u>oa</u>l o
m<u>ea</u>t e   b<u>ai</u>t a

36

The letter e at the end of a word can make the vowel in the middle long. For example, add e to the word pin to make pine. The short i sound in pin becomes a long vowel sound.

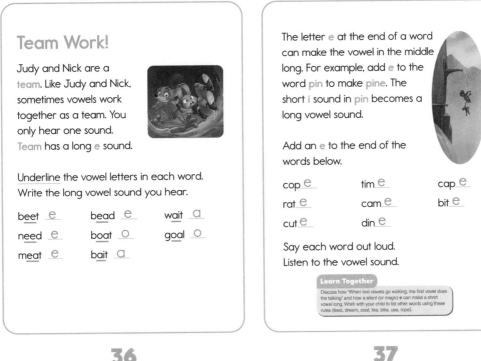

Add an e to the end of the words below.

cop e   tim e   cap e
rat e   cam e   bit e
cut e   din e

Say each word out loud. Listen to the vowel sound.

Learn Together
Discuss how "When two vowels go walking, the first vowel does the talking" and how a silent (or magic) e can make a short vowel long. Work with your child to list other words using these rules (feed, dream, coat, like, bike, use, rope).

37

© Disney

Answer Key

Fill in the missing sight words.

Rapunzel uses h e r hair to escape the tower.

Outside, s h e is filled with joy.

Flynn thinks t h e y should go back.

Rapunzel does not agree with h i m.

So h e comes up with a plan.

But is it the best plan for both of t h e m?

Learn Together
Help your child read the sight words, noting the letters they begin with and how long each word is. Your child can circle any other words they already know in the sentences.

39

Underline the sight words below.

Little Moana loves to play.

She can see a turtle on the beach.

Moana takes a closer look.

She helps the turtle make it to safety.

Moana can stop the birds from getting the turtle.

Learn Together
Help your child read each sentence, pausing at each sight word to let them read it. Make flash cards with some of the sight words (see the list in the glossary). Ask your child to read the words and use them in sentences.

41

Fill in the missing sight words.

Judy and Nick find s o m e clues.

Nick runs v e r y fast w i t h Judy.

Judy makes a call b e c a u s e they need help.

They tell the police t h a t they have new clues.

Learn Together
Ask your child to choose two sight words from this page. With your child, make up a sentence that includes the two words.

43

Fill in the missing sight words.

How w i l l Belle save the Beast?

Belle c a n save him with her love.

They will b e happy soon, after the Beast i s changed.

Belle and the Beast a r e in love.

Learn Together
On a blank piece of paper, create three columns. Label them characters, setting, and plot. With your child, fill out the columns with details from the story above.

45

© Disney

Rhyme Time

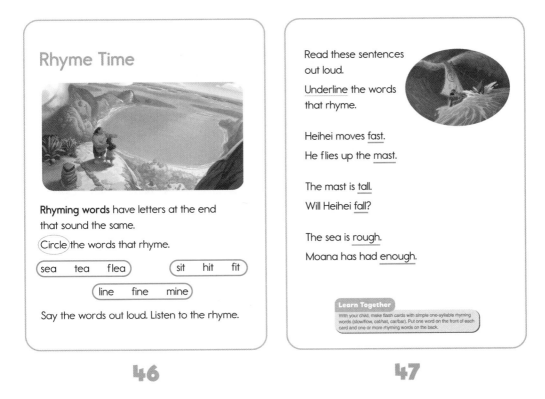

Rhyming words have letters at the end that sound the same.

Circle the words that rhyme.

| sea tea flea | | sit hit fit |
| line fine mine |

Say the words out loud. Listen to the rhyme.

46

Read these sentences out loud.

Underline the words that rhyme.

Heihei moves fast.
He flies up the mast.

The mast is tall.
Will Heihei fall?

The sea is rough.
Moana has had enough.

Learn Together
With your child, make flash cards with simple one-syllable rhyming words (slow/flow, cat/hat, car/bar). Put one word on the front of each card and one or more rhyming words on the back.

47

Words That Sound the Same

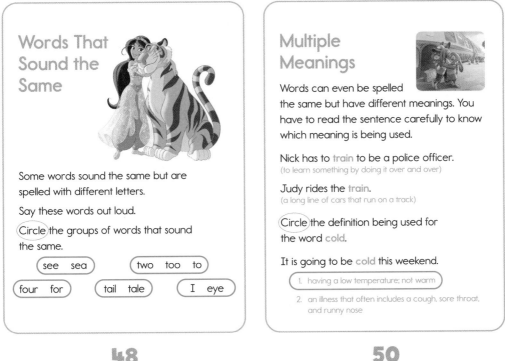

Some words sound the same but are spelled with different letters.

Say these words out loud.

Circle the groups of words that sound the same.

| see sea | two too to |
| four for | tail tale | I eye |

48

Multiple Meanings

Words can even be spelled the same but have different meanings. You have to read the sentence carefully to know which meaning is being used.

Nick has to train to be a police officer.
(to learn something by doing it over and over)

Judy rides the train.
(a long line of cars that run on a track)

Circle the definition being used for the word cold.

It is going to be cold this weekend.

1. having a low temperature; not warm

2. an illness that often includes a cough, sore throat, and runny nose

50

© Disney

51

Circle the correct definition of the colored word in each sentence.

Airplanes fly at high speeds.

> a small insect with two wings
>
> **to move through the air**

May I pet your dog?

> an animal that lives with people
>
> **to touch or stroke**

Swing the bat to hit the ball.

> a small, flying mammal
>
> **a wooden stick used in baseball**

Nick likes spending time in parks.

> **open, grassy areas for relaxing**
>
> stops and leaves a car

Learn Together

Give your child another word that has more than one meaning but the same spelling, like *fair* (equal or a place with rides and games). Have your child come up with a sentence for each meaning. Do this with other words as well.

52

Seeing Base Words

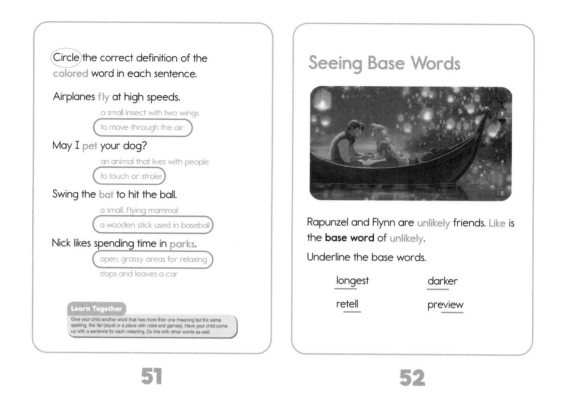

Rapunzel and Flynn are unlikely friends. Like is the **base word** of unlikely.

Underline the base words.

longest   darker

retell   preview

53

Match each new beginning to a base word.

re —— able
un —— read
(lines crossed)

Match each base word to a new ending.

sing —————— er

jump —————— ed

Learn Together

Explain to your child the meaning of **prefix** and **suffix**. Point to the new words created on this page as examples. *Re* and *un* are prefixes because they come at the beginning of the words, and *er* and *ed* are suffixes because they come at the end.

54

I Know Nouns

A noun names a person, place, or thing. A **proper noun** names a specific person, place, or thing. Proper nouns are capitalized. **Common nouns** are not.

Underline the proper nouns. Circle the common nouns.

Agrabah   (city)   (princess)

Aladdin   (monkey)   Abu

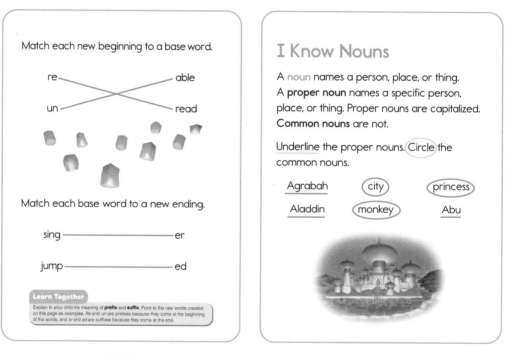

© Disne

Read the sentences below. (Circle) the proper nouns that should be capitalized.

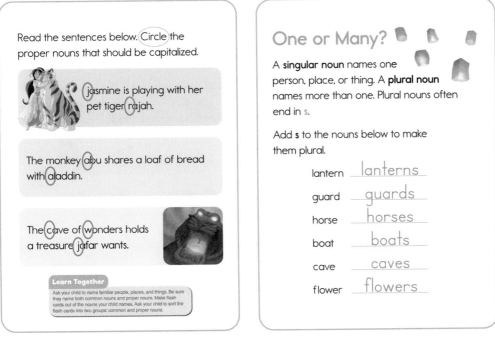

(j)asmine is playing with her pet tiger (r)ajah.

The monkey (a)bu shares a loaf of bread with (a)laddin.

The (c)ave of (w)onders holds a treasure (j)afar wants.

Learn Together
Ask your child to name familiar people, places, and things. Be sure they name both common nouns and proper nouns. Make flash cards out of the nouns your child names. Ask your child to sort the flash cards into two groups: common and proper nouns.

55

One or Many?

A **singular noun** names one person, place, or thing. A **plural noun** names more than one. Plural nouns often end in s.

Add **s** to the nouns below to make them plural.

lantern _lanterns_
guard _guards_
horse _horses_
boat _boats_
cave _caves_
flower _flowers_

56

Look at the pictures. (Circle) the correct singular or plural noun.

(pan)
pans

lantern
(lanterns)

paintbrush
(paintbrushes)

person
(people)

Learn Together
Ask your child to identify the singular and plural forms of other nouns that name things around you. Be sure to prompt the inclusion of some plural nouns that do not end in s, such as **children**, **feet**, or **mice**.

57

Whose Is That?

Make the nouns below **possessive** by adding 's.

Moana _'s_ boat
Maui _'s_ fishhook
Motunui _'s_ chief
Te Fiti _'s_ heart
The ocean _'s_ chosen one

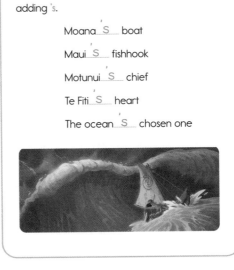

58

© Disney

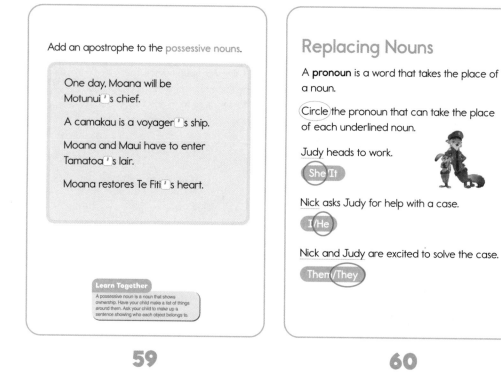

Add an apostrophe to the possessive nouns.

One day, Moana will be Motunui's chief.

A camakau is a voyager's ship.

Moana and Maui have to enter Tamatoa's lair.

Moana restores Te Fiti's heart.

Learn Together
A possessive noun is a noun that shows ownership. Have your child make a list of things around them. Ask your child to make up a sentence showing who each object belongs to.

59

Replacing Nouns

A **pronoun** is a word that takes the place of a noun.

Circle the pronoun that can take the place of each underlined noun.

Judy heads to work.

She / It

Nick asks Judy for help with a case.

I / He

Nick and Judy are excited to solve the case.

Them / They

60

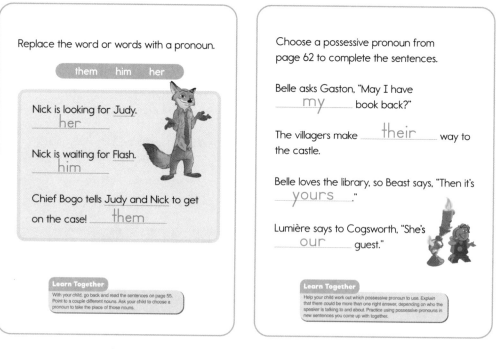

Replace the word or words with a pronoun.

them   him   her

Nick is looking for Judy.
her

Nick is waiting for Flash.
him

Chief Bogo tells Judy and Nick to get on the case! them

Learn Together
With your child, go back and read the sentences on page 55. Point to a couple different nouns. Ask your child to choose a pronoun to take the place of those nouns.

61

Choose a possessive pronoun from page 62 to complete the sentences.

Belle asks Gaston, "May I have my book back?"

The villagers make their way to the castle.

Belle loves the library, so Beast says, "Then it's yours."

Lumière says to Cogsworth, "She's our guest."

Learn Together
Help your child work out which possessive pronoun to use. Explain that there could be more than one right answer, depending on who the speaker is talking to and about. Practice using possessive pronouns in new sentences you come up with together.

63

228

© Disney

Match each sentence to the correct ending.

Rajah
bite a suitor's pants.
bites a suitor's pants.

Jafar
tricks the sultan.
trick the sultan.

The guards
captures Aladdin.
capture Aladdin.

Learn Together
Create sentences about your child or about both of you. Have your child fill in the correct verb that agrees with the subject.

65

Read the sentences below. Circle the present tense verbs, draw a box around the past tense verbs, and underline the future tense verbs.

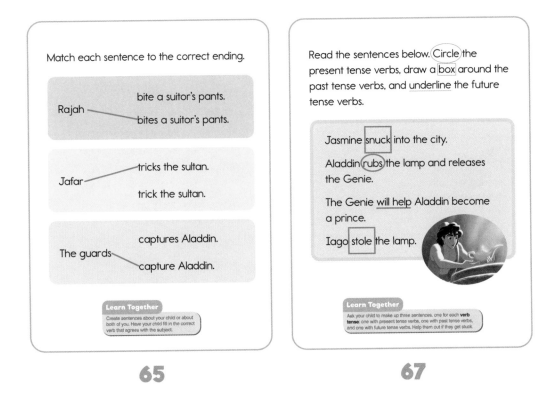

Jasmine snuck into the city.

Aladdin rubs the lamp and releases the Genie.

The Genie will help Aladdin become a prince.

Iago stole the lamp.

Learn Together
Ask your child to make up three sentences, one for each **verb tense**: one with present tense verbs, one with past tense verbs, and one with future tense verbs. Help them out if they get stuck.

67

Combining Sentences

Sometimes, sentences can be combined.

The table was set.
The table was filled with food.

Both sentences tell about the table. You can combine the sentences using and.

The table was set and filled with food.

Place a check mark next to the sentences that use and.

☐ Lumiére likes to sing.
☐ Lumiére likes to dance.
☑ Lumiére likes to sing and dance.

☐ Beast is kind.
☑ Beast and Mrs. Potts are kind.
☐ Mrs. Potts is kind.

68

Combine each pair of sentences into one sentence. Write the new sentence.

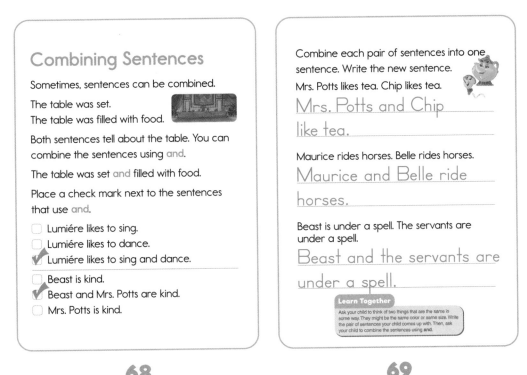

Mrs. Potts likes tea. Chip likes tea.

Mrs. Potts and Chip like tea.

Maurice rides horses. Belle rides horses.

Maurice and Belle ride horses.

Beast is under a spell. The servants are under a spell.

Beast and the servants are under a spell.

Learn Together
Ask your child to think of two things that are the same in some way. They might be the same color or same size. Write the pair of sentences your child comes up with. Then, ask your child to combine the sentences using **and**.

69

© Disney

Answer Key

(Circle) what Rapunzel is looking at.

Describe how Rapunzel is feeling.

Rapunzel is sad that
Flynn is sailing away.

Describe the setting.

It is night time, by the
water.

Answers will vary.
Sample answers are shown.

Learn Together
With your child, examine and discuss this picture. What else does
your child notice? When you read books together, encourage your
child to use the picture clues to help them understand the story.

71

Moana and Heihei are on the boat.

The waves are very big.

Heihei holds on tightly.

They do their best to stay afloat as
they flee from Te Kā.

The waves are getting higher.

Answers will vary.
Sample answers:

How would you feel if you were on the
boat with Moana and Heihei? Why?

I would be frightened
because the monster is
scary.

Learn Together
Read the story to your child. Help your child **make connections** and
respond to the questions. Ask your child to recall a time when they were
challenged (swimming for the first time). How did they feel?

73

The Beast becomes a prince.

The prince is a tall man.

He has brown hair and a kind smile.

Belle wears a yellow dress to dance
with him.

The prince is very gentle with Belle.

Underline the clues in the story that help
you answer these questions.

Is the prince tall or short?

What does Belle wear for their dance?

Learn Together
With your child, describe what a favorite character
from a book or movie looks like.

75

Order! Order!

Put the story back in order.

Number the boxes in the order the
story happened.

2

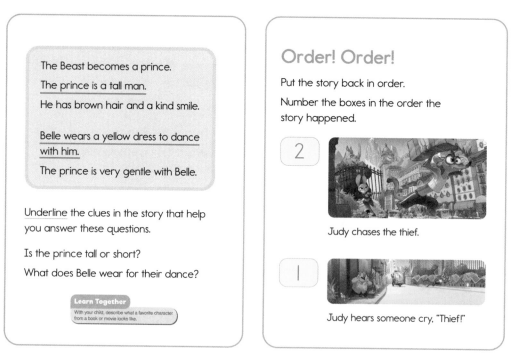

Judy chases the thief.

1

Judy hears someone cry, "Thief!"

80

230

© Disney

4

Finally, she gets the weasel
and brings him to the station.

3

There are small rodents everywhere,
and Judy has to dodge them.

Learn Together
Help your child figure out the story order. Find other
pictures for your child to put in order. Encourage them
to sequence other objects or actions.

81

Fish, turtles, crabs, and many other
animals live in the coral reefs.

Coral reefs provide shelter and
food to these animals.

Many of the animals in the
Polynesian reef do not live
anywhere else in the world.

Answers will vary.
Sample answers:

Write one fact you learned about reefs.

Coral reefs provide
shelter.

Learn Together
Read this **nonfiction text** to your child. Ask your child
what differences there are between this text and the
fiction text on pages 77 and 78.

83

Where Do I Go?

Maps are pictures that can tell you what a
community looks like.

Path will vary.

Trace a path from the A in Tundratown
to the B in the Rainforest District.

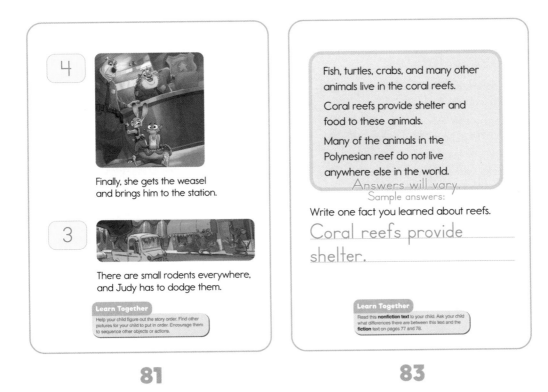

The Regions of Zootopia

■ Rainforest District ■ Tundratown ■ Sahara Square ■ Savanna Central

84

The magic carpet is made of (soft,)
colorful wool.

It is purple with gold and
red patterns.

It can move on its own!

When it flies, it rustles and hums,
soaring and diving.

Underline the words that describe what
the magic carpet looks like.

(Circle) a word that describes what
the carpet feels like.

Learn Together
These description words are **adjectives**. What
other adjectives would your child add? Your child
can try describing Aladdin or Abu.

87

© Disney

What Is the Title?

A title tells you what a story is about.

Books, poems, movies, and plays all have titles.

The title of this book is *Belle to the Rescue*.

Write another title for this book.

Answers will vary. Sample answer:
Belle Goes Skating

90

Look at this picture.

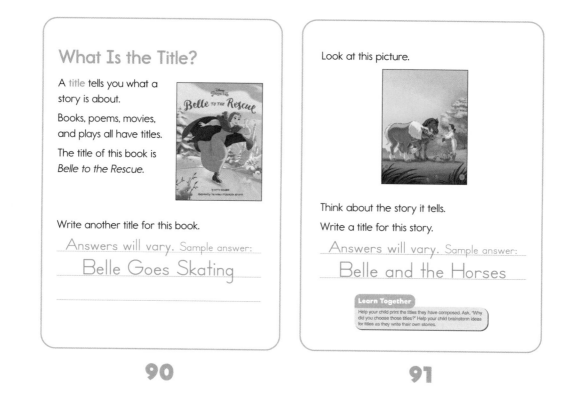

Think about the story it tells.

Write a title for this story.

Answers will vary. Sample answer:
Belle and the Horses

Learn Together
Help your child print the titles they have composed. Ask, "Why did you choose those titles?" Help your child brainstorm ideas for titles as they write their own stories.

91

Label this picture.

car   light

tire   Judy

Learn Together
Help your child label this picture, naming each object to label, sounding out the word, and helping them spell it. With your child, draw a picture of a neighborhood park and label it.

93

Write a caption for each picture.

The sea moves Moana.

Moana sails away.

Answers will vary.
Sample answers are shown.

Learn Together
With your child, draw a picture. Discuss what is happening in it. Write a caption for the picture.

95

© Disney

Lots of Sentences

A sentence tells you something.

A sentence can have different kinds of punctuation.

Belle likes to read books.

A sentence starts with a capital letter.

This sentence ends with a period.

Write a sentence about something you like to do. Answers will vary.
Sample answers:
End the sentence with a period.

I like to play with my dog.

96

A sentence can ask a question.

A sentence can also show excitement.

Where is Belle going?

A question ends with a question mark.

Belle rides fast!

An exclamation mark shows excitement.

Write a sentence that asks a question.

What is Belle reading?

Write a sentence that shows excitement.

That looks fun!

Answers will vary.
Sample answers are shown.

Learn Together
Help your child write different sentences about your family. One sentence can end with a period, another with a question mark, and the third with an exclamation point.

97

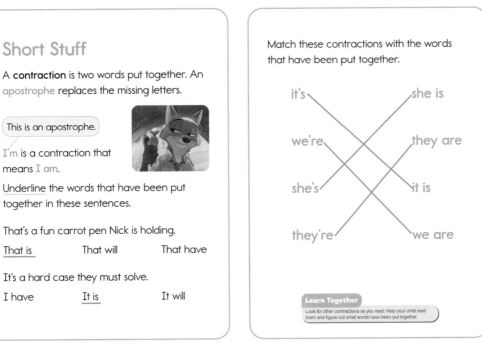

Short Stuff

A **contraction** is two words put together. An apostrophe replaces the missing letters.

This is an apostrophe.

I'm is a contraction that means I am.

Underline the words that have been put together in these sentences.

That's a fun carrot pen Nick is holding.

<u>That is</u>   That will   That have

It's a hard case they must solve.

I have   <u>It is</u>   It will

104

Match these contractions with the words that have been put together.

it's — she is
we're — they are
she's — it is
they're — we are

Learn Together
Look for other contractions as you read. Help your child read them and figure out what words have been put together.

105

© Disney

Write 0 above the empty containers.

Learn Together
Make sure your child has an understanding of zero. Provide them with opportunities to discuss how there are zero cookies left in the box or zero toys on the floor.

107

One to One

Aladdin and Jasmine each have good friends.

Draw a line from Aladdin and Jasmine to their friends.

108

Draw a line to match each picture on the left with a picture on the right.

Learn Together
Help your child identify other common examples of **one-to-one correspondence**. Match one bowl to one spoon or one mitten to its mate.

109

On the Line

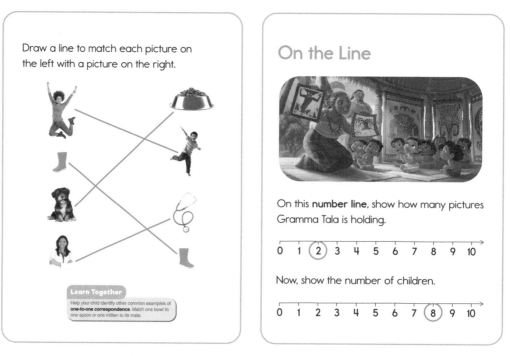

On this **number line**, show how many pictures Gramma Tala is holding.

0 1 (2) 3 4 5 6 7 8 9 10

Now, show the number of children.

0 1 2 3 4 5 6 7 (8) 9 10

122

© Disney

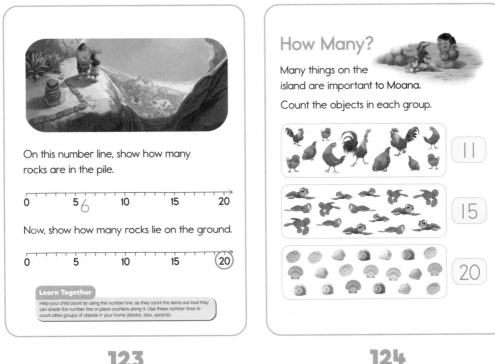

On this number line, show how many rocks are in the pile.

0   5 6   10   15   20

Now, show how many rocks lie on the ground.

0   5   10   15   (20)

Learn Together

Help your child count by using the number line; as they count the items out loud they can shade the number line or place counters along it. Use these number lines to count other groups of objects in your home (blocks, toys, spoons).

123

How Many?

Many things on the island are important to Moana.

Count the objects in each group.

11

15

20

124

Trace each number below.

Draw that number of objects in the box.

14

17

12

Learn Together

With your child, collect groups of 11 to 20 objects (buttons, crayons, toy cars). Ask, "How many do you have?"

125

Count Them All!

Belle's father, Maurice, needs a lot of equipment to make inventions.

Count the objects in each group.

18

11

126

© Disney

On the left, draw 15 objects that Maurice could use in his inventions.

Draw more objects on the right to make 20.

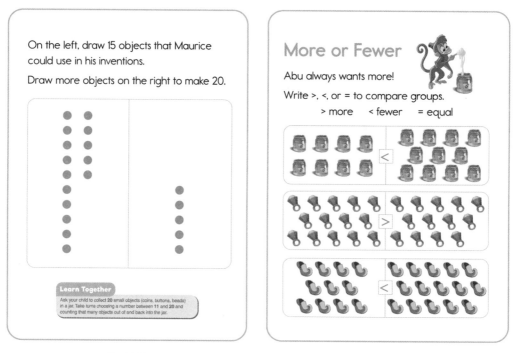

Learn Together

Ask your child to collect 20 small objects (coins, buttons, beads) in a jar. Take turns choosing a number between 11 and 20 and counting that many objects out of and back into the jar.

127

More or Fewer

Abu always wants more!

Write >, <, or = to compare groups.

> more   < fewer   = equal

128

Here are more of Abu's collections!

Count the objects in each group.

Write >, <, or = to compare groups.

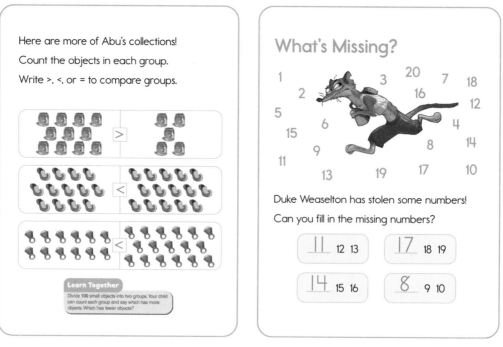

Learn Together

Divide 100 small objects into two groups. Your child can count each group and say which has more objects. Which has fewer objects?

129

What's Missing?

1   2   3   20   7   18
5   16   12
15   6   4
9   8   14
11   17   10
13   19

Duke Weaselton has stolen some numbers!

Can you fill in the missing numbers?

| 11 | 12 | 13 |

| 17 | 18 | 19 |

| 14 | 15 | 16 |

| 8 | 9 | 10 |

130

© Disney

131

12 13 **14**	15 16 **17**
18 19 **20**	13 14 **15**
16 17 **18**	9 10 **11**
11 12 **13**	17 18 **19**
7 8 **9**	10 11 **12**
14 15 **16**	8 9 **10**

Learn Together

Using **100** objects, make a group (27 crayons or 38 grapes). Your child can count them out loud. Add 1 more and ask how many there are now.

131

I Think There Are...

Sometimes, you can guess, or estimate, how many objects you see.

Estimate the number of coconuts.

Estimates will vary.

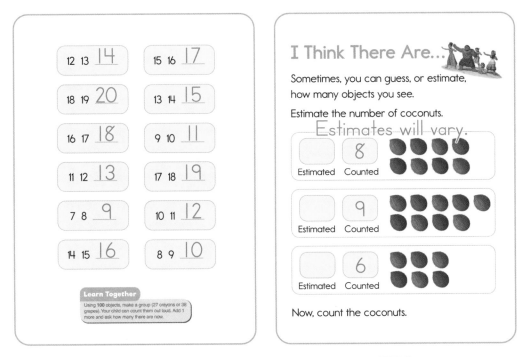

Estimated   Counted **8**

Estimated   Counted **9**

Estimated   Counted **6**

Now, count the coconuts.

132

Estimate the number of cubes.

Estimates will vary.

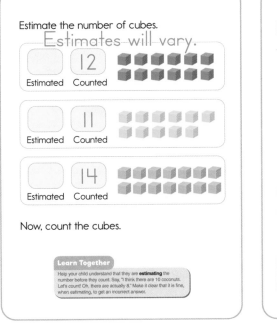

Estimated   Counted **12**

Estimated   Counted **11**

Estimated   Counted **14**

Now, count the cubes.

Learn Together

Help your child understand that they are **estimating** the number before they count. Say, "I think there are 10 coconuts. Let's count! Oh, there are actually 8." Make it clear that it is fine, when estimating, to get an incorrect answer.

133

First, Second, Third

These mice are running away.

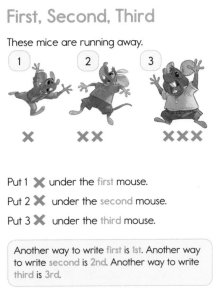

1   2   3

✗   ✗✗   ✗✗✗

Put 1 ✗ under the first mouse.

Put 2 ✗ under the second mouse.

Put 3 ✗ under the third mouse.

Another way to write first is 1st. Another way to write second is 2nd. Another way to write third is 3rd.

134

© Disney

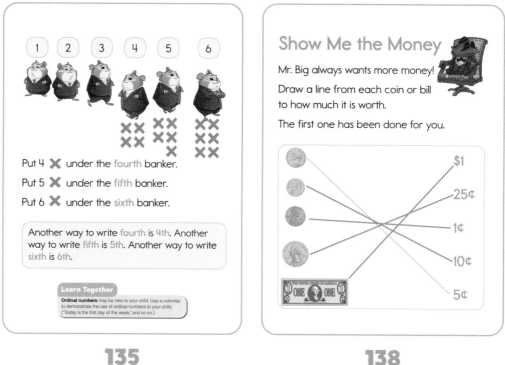

Put 4 ✖ under the fourth banker.
Put 5 ✖ under the fifth banker.
Put 6 ✖ under the sixth banker.

Another way to write fourth is 4th. Another way to write fifth is 5th. Another way to write sixth is 6th.

Learn Together
Ordinal numbers may be new to your child. Use a calendar to demonstrate the use of ordinal numbers to your child. ("Today is the first day of the week," and so on.)

135

Show Me the Money

Mr. Big always wants more money!

Draw a line from each coin or bill to how much it is worth.

The first one has been done for you.

$1
25¢
1¢
10¢
5¢

138

Show 5¢.

Answers will vary.
Sample answers are shown.

Show 10¢ in two different ways.

or

Show 20¢ in two different ways.

or

Learn Together
Play "Store" with your child using real money and price tags for some small toys. Take turns shopping and paying.

139

Sort It Out!

Moana sees many fish when she swims.

Circle all the fish with yellow fins.

Underline all the fish without yellow fins.

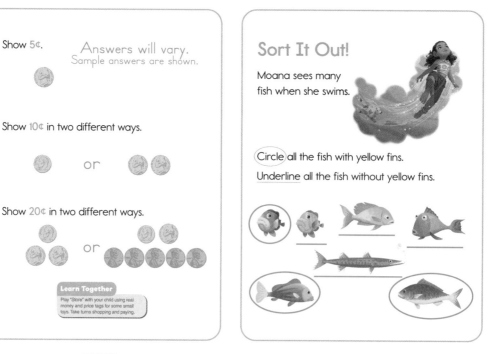

140

© Disney

What's the Pattern?

In the Cave of Wonders, Aladdin sees objects arranged in patterns.

What comes next in each pattern?

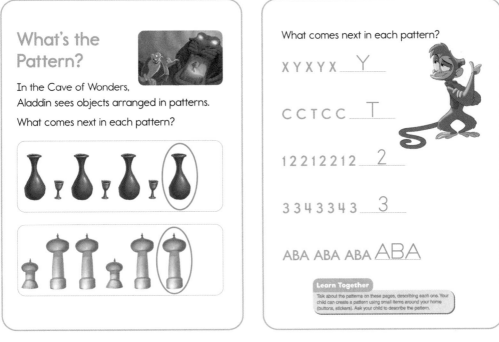

142

What comes next in each pattern?

X Y X Y X __Y__

C C T C C __T__

1 2 2 1 2 2 1 2 __2__

3 3 4 3 3 4 3 __3__

ABA ABA ABA __ABA__

Learn Together

Talk about the patterns on these pages, describing each one. Your child can create a pattern using small items around your home (buttons, stickers). Ask your child to describe the pattern.

143

Making Patterns

Mrs. Potts's base has a pattern. Color the objects below to complete the pattern.

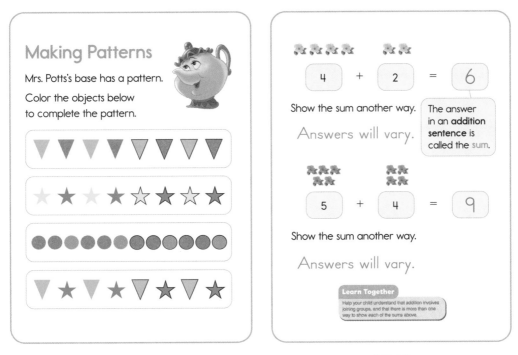

144

4 + 2 = 6

Show the sum another way.

Answers will vary.

> The answer in an **addition sentence** is called the sum.

5 + 4 = 9

Show the sum another way.

Answers will vary.

Learn Together

Help your child understand that addition involves joining groups, and that there is more than one way to show each of the sums above.

147

© Disney

Answer Key

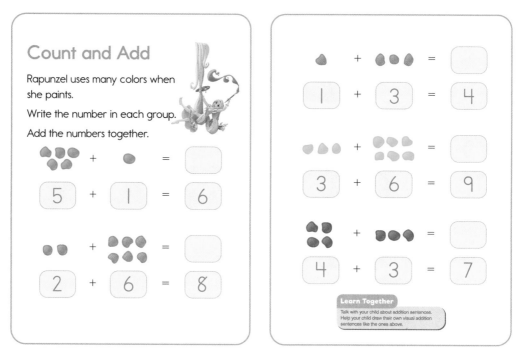

Count and Add

Rapunzel uses many colors when she paints.

Write the number in each group.

Add the numbers together.

5 + 1 = 6

2 + 6 = 8

1 + 3 = 4

3 + 6 = 9

4 + 3 = 7

Learn Together
Talk with your child about addition sentences. Help your child draw their own visual addition sentences like the ones above.

148

149

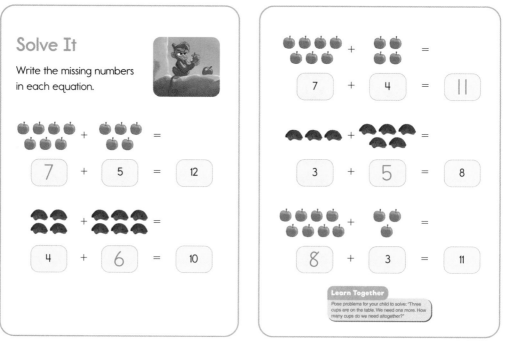

Solve It

Write the missing numbers in each equation.

7 + 5 = 12

4 + 6 = 10

7 + 4 = 11

3 + 5 = 8

8 + 3 = 11

Learn Together
Pose problems for your child to solve: "Three cups are on the table. We need one more. How many cups do we need altogether?"

150

151

© Disney

Add Them Up

Judy Hopps has a big family.

Judy's parents and 5 brothers visit her in Zootopia.

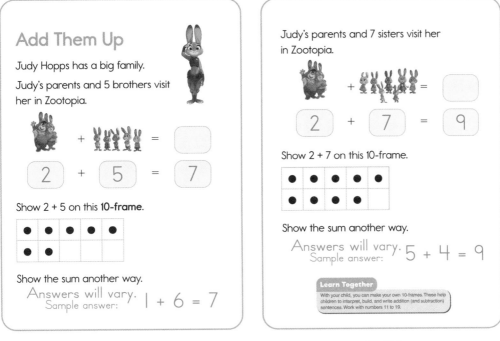

$2 + 5 = 7$

Show 2 + 5 on this **10-frame**.

Show the sum another way.

Answers will vary.
Sample answer: $1 + 6 = 7$

152

Judy's parents and 7 sisters visit her in Zootopia.

$2 + 7 = 9$

Show 2 + 7 on this 10-frame.

Show the sum another way.

Answers will vary.
Sample answer: $5 + 4 = 9$

Learn Together

With your child, you can make your own 10-frames. These help children to interpret, build, and write addition (and subtraction) sentences. Work with numbers 11 to 19.

153

Solve the 3-number problems.

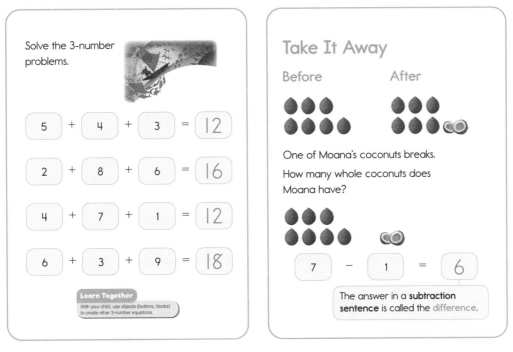

$5 + 4 + 3 = 12$

$2 + 8 + 6 = 16$

$4 + 7 + 1 = 12$

$6 + 3 + 9 = 18$

Learn Together

With your child, use objects (buttons, blocks) to create other 3-number equations.

155

Take It Away

Before   **After**

One of Moana's coconuts breaks.

How many whole coconuts does Moana have?

$7 - 1 = 6$

The answer in a **subtraction sentence** is called the difference.

156

© Disney

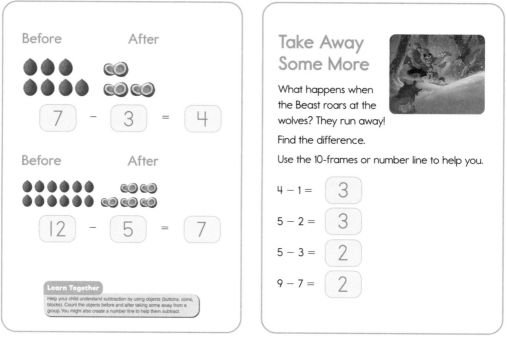

Before   After

7 − 3 = 4

Before   After

12 − 5 = 7

Learn Together

Help your child understand subtraction by using objects (buttons, coins, blocks). Count the objects before and after taking some away from a group. You might also create a number line to help them subtract.

157

Take Away Some More

What happens when the Beast roars at the wolves? They run away!

Find the difference.

Use the 10-frames or number line to help you.

4 − 1 = 3

5 − 2 = 3

5 − 3 = 2

9 − 7 = 2

158

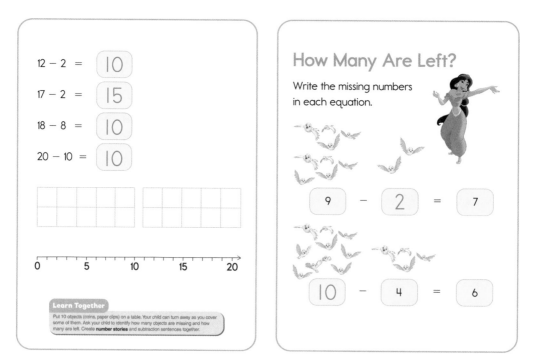

12 − 2 = 10

17 − 2 = 15

18 − 8 = 10

20 − 10 = 10

0   5   10   15   20

Learn Together

Put 10 objects (coins, paper clips) on a table. Your child can turn away as you cover some of them. Ask your child to identify how many objects are missing and how many are left. Create **number stories** and subtraction sentences together.

159

How Many Are Left?

Write the missing numbers in each equation.

9 − 2 = 7

10 − 4 = 6

160

242

© Disney

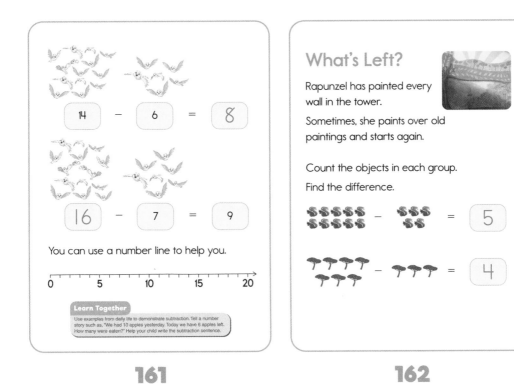

$14 - 6 = 8$

$16 - 7 = 9$

You can use a number line to help you.

0   5   10   15   20

Learn Together
Use examples from daily life to demonstrate subtraction. Tell a number story such as, "We had 10 apples yesterday. Today we have 6 apples left. How many were eaten?" Help your child write the subtraction sentence.

161

What's Left?

Rapunzel has painted every wall in the tower.

Sometimes, she paints over old paintings and starts again.

Count the objects in each group. Find the difference.

$= 5$

$= 4$

162

Look at the 10-frames.

Write the number in each 10-frame in a blank box.

Find the difference.

$9 - 7 = 2$

$10 - 5 = 5$

Learn Together
Rather than drawing 10-frames, your child could use connecting blocks in groups of 10. Your child can create number stories for subtraction, disconnecting the indicated number of blocks.

163

Who's Lying?

Nick is trying to figure out if these equations are telling the truth. Help him by writing true by the equations that are correct and false by the equations that are wrong.

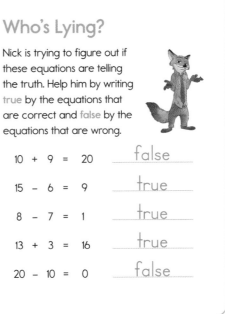

$10 + 9 = 20$ _false_

$15 - 6 = 9$ _true_

$8 - 7 = 1$ _true_

$13 + 3 = 16$ _true_

$20 - 10 = 0$ _false_

164

© Disney

Answer Key

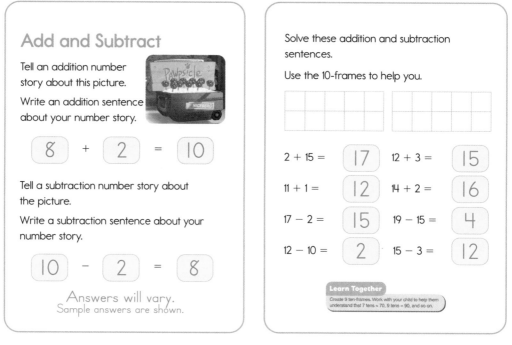

Add and Subtract

Tell an addition number story about this picture.

Write an addition sentence about your number story.

$$8 + 2 = 10$$

Tell a subtraction number story about the picture.

Write a subtraction sentence about your number story.

$$10 - 2 = 8$$

Answers will vary.
Sample answers are shown.

166

Solve these addition and subtraction sentences.

Use the 10-frames to help you.

$2 + 15 = \boxed{17}$ $12 + 3 = \boxed{15}$

$11 + 1 = \boxed{12}$ $14 + 2 = \boxed{16}$

$17 - 2 = \boxed{15}$ $19 - 15 = \boxed{4}$

$12 - 10 = \boxed{2}$ $15 - 3 = \boxed{12}$

Learn Together

Create 9 ten-frames. Work with your child to help them understand that 7 tens = 70, 9 tens = 90, and so on.

167

Add within 100

Moana needs help adding the coconuts being collected in Motunui. Solve the addition problems to help her!

```
  26        14        32
+  6      +  8      +  2
  32        22        34

  11        80        51
+  9      +  5      +  4
  20        85        55

  43        68        77
+  3      +  6      +  1
  46        74        78
```

168

The voyagers just brought back the fish they caught. Help Moana add them up!

```
  65        14        47
+ 10      + 20      + 10
  75        34        57

  82        26        53
+ 10      + 30      + 20
  92        56        73

  31        48        79
+ 30      + 10      + 10
  61        58        89
```

Learn Together

Help your child with the two-digit addition problems. Have them practice two-digit addition further by asking them to find 10 more than a number or by writing more addition problems for them to solve.

169

244

© Disney

Subtract

Duke Weaselton has been busy! He needs help subtracting how many movies he's sold so he knows how many he has left.

60 −10 **50**	30 −10 **20**	40 −10 **30**
70 −10 **60**	50 −10 **40**	10 −10 **0**
90 −10 **80**	80 −10 **70**	20 −10 **10**

Now help Finnick! Subtract the pawpsicles he's sold from his total number of pawpsicles.

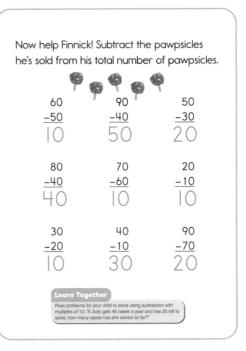

60 −50 **10**	90 −40 **50**	50 −30 **20**
80 −40 **40**	70 −60 **10**	20 −10 **10**
30 −20 **10**	40 −10 **30**	90 −70 **20**

Learn Together

Pose problems for your child to solve using subtraction with multiples of 10: "If Judy gets 40 cases a year and has 20 left to solve, how many cases has she solved so far?"

How Long?

These drums come in different sizes.

How many blocks long are these drums?

3

6

How many paper clips long are these objects?

Toothpaste   6

4

Draw an object that is 7 paper clips long.

Learn Together

Try measuring real objects around your home by using other **non-standard units** (straws, strips of paper of equal lengths, erasers).

© Disney

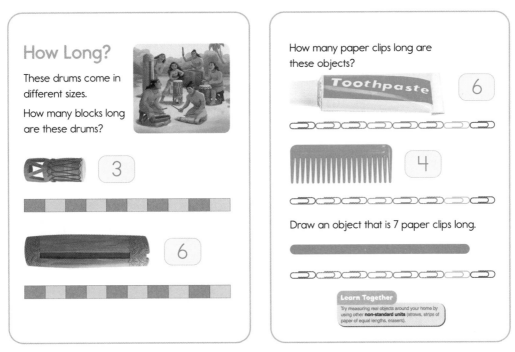

Answer Key

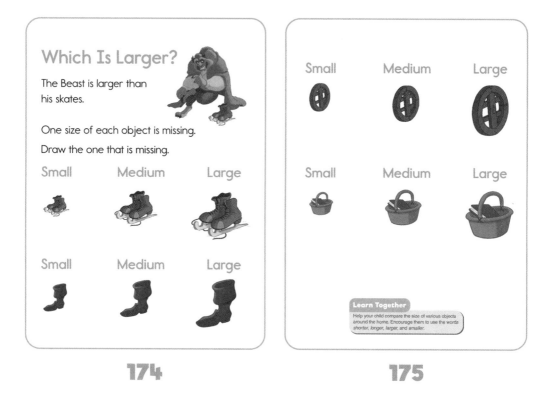

Which Is Larger?

The Beast is larger than his skates.

One size of each object is missing.
Draw the one that is missing.

Small   Medium   Large

Small   Medium   Large

174

Small   Medium   Large

Small   Medium   Large

Learn Together
Help your child compare the size of various objects around the home. Encourage them to use the words shorter, longer, larger, and smaller.

175

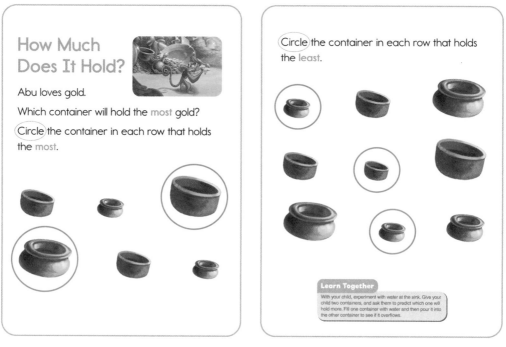

How Much Does It Hold?

Abu loves gold.

Which container will hold the most gold?
Circle the container in each row that holds the most.

176

Circle the container in each row that holds the least.

Learn Together
With your child, experiment with water at the sink. Give your child two containers, and ask them to predict which one will hold more. Fill one container with water and then pour it into the other container to see if it overflows.

177

246

© Disney

Which Holds More?

Nick is on the hustle, but he needs to figure out which container holds more.

Circle the one in each row that holds more.

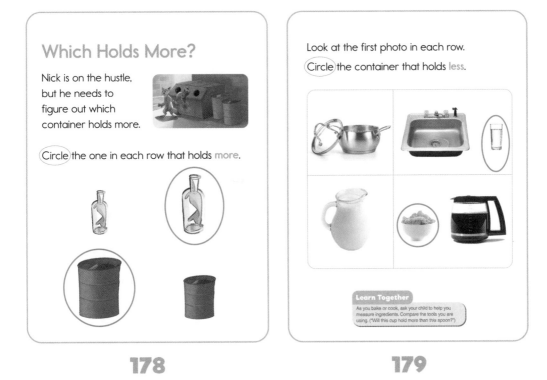

178

Look at the first photo in each row.

Circle the container that holds less.

Learn Together

As you bake or cook, ask your child to help you measure ingredients. Compare the tools you are using. ("Will this cup hold more than this spoon?")

179

Which One Is Heavier?

Which one is heavier?

Circle the one that is heavier.

180

Which One Is Lighter?

Pua and Heihei are having fun!

Circle the one in each box that is lighter.

182

© Disney

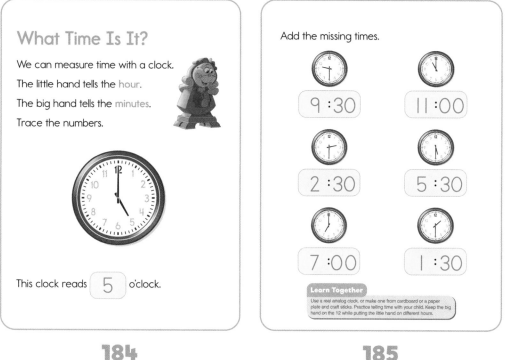

What Time Is It?

We can measure time with a clock.

The little hand tells the hour.

The big hand tells the minutes.

Trace the numbers.

This clock reads **5** o'clock.

Add the missing times.

9 :30   **11** :00

2 :30   **5** :30

7 :00   **1** :30

Learn Together

Use a real analog clock, or make one from cardboard or a paper plate and craft sticks. Practice telling time with your child. Keep the big hand on the 12 while putting the little hand on different hours.

184   **185**

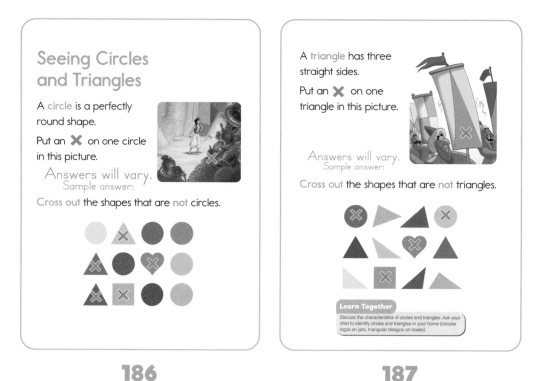

Seeing Circles and Triangles

A circle is a perfectly round shape.

Put an ✖ on one circle in this picture.

Answers will vary.
Sample answer:

Cross out the shapes that are not circles.

A triangle has three straight sides.

Put an ✖ on one triangle in this picture.

Answers will vary.
Sample answer:

Cross out the shapes that are not triangles.

Learn Together

Discuss the characteristics of circles and triangles. Ask your child to identify circles and triangles in your home (circular logos on jars, triangular designs on boxes).

186   **187**

© Disney

Looking for Rectangles and Squares

A rectangle has four sides.

Two sides are longer than the other two sides.

(Circle) one rectangle in this picture.

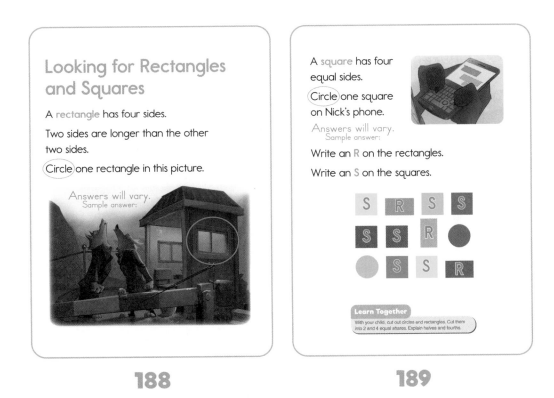

Answers will vary.
Sample answer:

A square has four equal sides.

(Circle) one square on Nick's phone.

Answers will vary.
Sample answer:

Write an R on the rectangles.

Write an S on the squares.

S	R	S	S
S	S	R	●
●	S	S	R

Learn Together
With your child, cut out circles and rectangles. Cut them into 2 and 4 equal shares. Explain halves and fourths.

188

189

What's That Shape?

A pentagon has five sides.

The Sultan's blue ring is shaped like a pentagon.

Cross out the shapes that are not pentagons.

A hexagon has six sides.

Look at the hexagons on this gem.

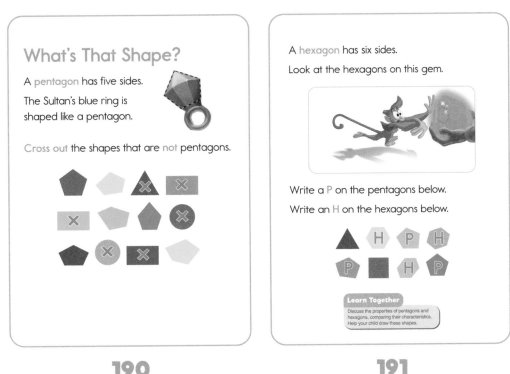

Write a P on the pentagons below.

Write an H on the hexagons below.

▲	H	P	H
P	■	H	P

Learn Together
Discuss the properties of pentagons and hexagons, comparing their characteristics. Help your child draw these shapes.

190

191

© Disney

Solid Objects

This object is called a sphere.

Circle the sphere on the sword.

Cross out the objects that are not spheres.

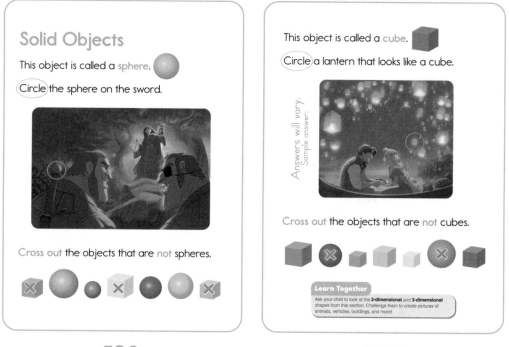

192

This object is called a cube.

Circle a lantern that looks like a cube.

Answers will vary.
Sample answer:

Cross out the objects that are not cubes.

Learn Together

Ask your child to look at the **2-dimensional** and **3-dimensional** shapes from this section. Challenge them to create pictures of animals, vehicles, buildings, and more!

193

More Solid Objects

This object is called a cylinder.

The bottoms of these towers are shaped like cylinders. Circle one of the cylinders.

Answers will vary.
Sample answer:

Cross out the objects that are not cylinders.

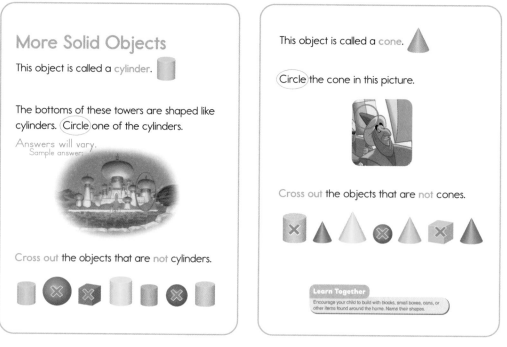

194

This object is called a cone.

Circle the cone in this picture.

Cross out the objects that are not cones.

Learn Together

Encourage your child to build with blocks, small boxes, cans, or other items found around the home. Name their shapes.

195

250

© Disney

Words for Where

Some words tell us where people or objects are.

Match each resident of Zootopia to the correct word.

in front

on

behind

Look at this picture.

(Circle) something that is above.

Underline something that is between.

Answers will vary. Sample answer:

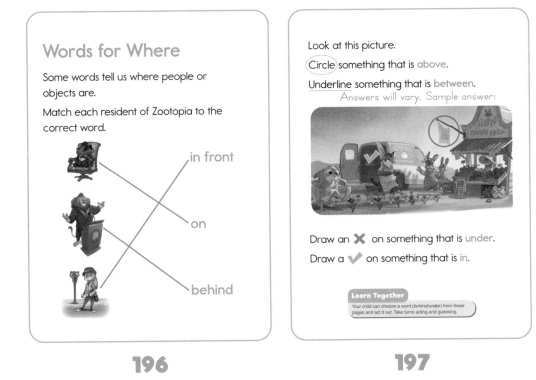

Draw an ✖ on something that is under.

Draw a ✔ on something that is in.

Learn Together

Your child can choose a word (behind/under) from these pages and act it out. Take turns acting and guessing.

196

197

Same or Different?

The Stabbington Brothers look alike in many ways.

But they also look different.

Answers will vary.
Sample answers:

How do they look alike?

They are both wearing brown boots and green vests.

How do they look different?

Only one brother has an eye patch.

(Circle) the objects in each group that are the same.

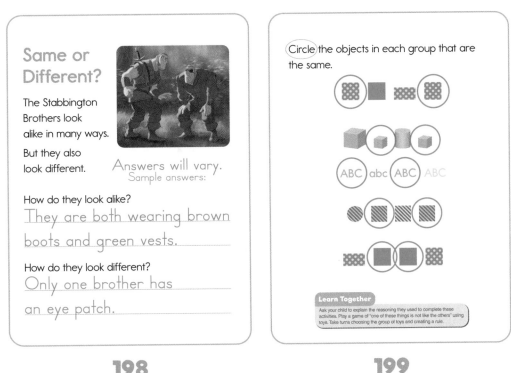

Learn Together

Ask your child to explain the reasoning they used to complete these activities. Play a game of "one of these things is not like the others" using toys. Take turns choosing the group of toys and creating a rule.

198

199

© Disney

Answer Key

What Belongs?

Circle the objects in each group that go together.

Look at the first picture in each row.
Circle the other picture that is the same.

Learn Together
Your child can collect 15 small objects and sort them by color, shape, or another attribute.

200

201

Find the Rule!

Cross out the one in each group that does not belong.

Answers will vary.
Sample answers:

Rule: need to be wearing blue

Rule: need to be wearing a dress

Look at the first picture in each row.
Decide if it belongs in the group on the right.
Cross it out if it does not belong.
Circle it if it does belong.

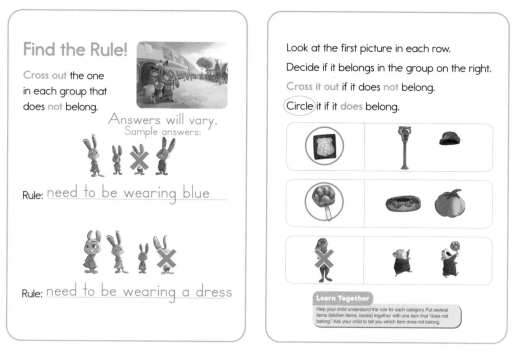

Learn Together
Help your child understand the rule for each category. Put several items (kitchen items, books) together with one item that "does not belong." Ask your child to tell you which item does not belong.

202

203

252

© Disney

Sort It!

Rapunzel's room needs cleaning up.

Put a 1 beside the objects that go in Basket 1.

Put a 2 beside the objects that go in Basket 2.

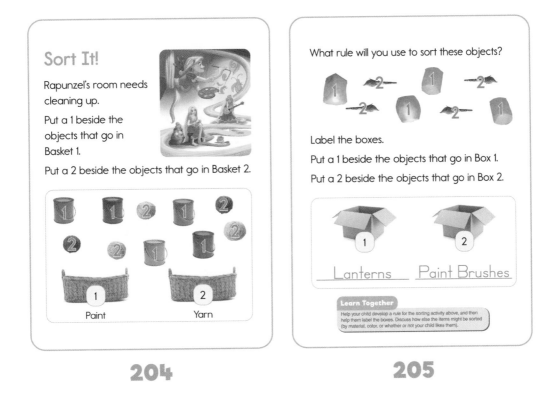

Paint

Yarn

What rule will you use to sort these objects?

Label the boxes.

Put a 1 beside the objects that go in Box 1.

Put a 2 beside the objects that go in Box 2.

1 Lanterns

2 Paint Brushes

Learn Together

Help your child develop a rule for the sorting activity above, and then help them label the boxes. Discuss how else the items might be sorted (by material, color, or whether or not your child likes them).

204

205

© Disney

Look at all the yarn Rapunzel has!
Create a picture graph.

Rapunzel's Yarn

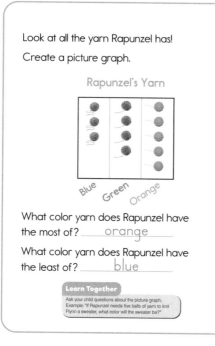

Blue   Green   Orange

What color yarn does Rapunzel have
the most of? _____orange_____

What color yarn does Rapunzel have
the least of? _____blue_____

Learn Together
Ask your child questions about the picture graph.
Example: "If Rapunzel needs five balls of yarn to knit
Flynn a sweater, what color will the sweater be?"

209

Create a picture graph.

License Plates

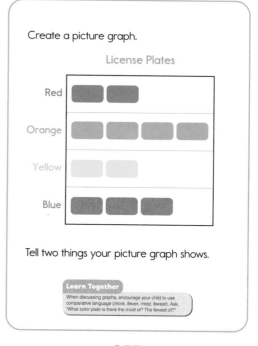

Tell two things your picture graph shows.

Learn Together
When discussing graphs, encourage your child to use
comparative language (*more, fewer, most, fewest*). Ask,
"What color plate is there the most of? The fewest of?"

211

© Disney

Congratulations

to

_____

for completing this workbook!
Keep up the good work!

© Disney